I0526059

SIREN
OF
SILENCE

INDIE
BACK
PRESS

1

<u>BOOK FOUR</u>

Trigger Warning

This book contains potentially triggering content, including (but not limited to) sexual assault, slavery, abduction, violence, and death. Reader discretion is advised.

Deadication

Be a good little bookworm and spread your pages for me. Or shall I make you beg first?

3

Immortal World

Book 4: Siren of Silence

Prologue

Theia...

From the moment my sisters and I were locked in the cage after leaving our island, one soldier's gaze was constant. He never stopped looking at me, and I recognized the look in his eye. It was the same predatory gleam I'd seen on the faces of my aunts and even my mother when they lured men to the island. Our island, with its dramatic rocky cliffs crowned by vibrant red and pink hibiscus and waters so impossibly clear you could see the ocean floor beneath, felt like a distant dream. While his eyes burned with hunger and desire, mine met his with a mixture of disgust and a desperate attempt to conceal my fear.

4

The rocking of the ship, paired with the creaking noise, had replaced the soft sound of waves brushing the shore. The melody of wild birds was drowned out by the rhythmic thud of men walking upon the wooden planks above our heads. The soft sand and grass we once rested on had been stolen from us, replaced by straw so rough it pricked my skin. The metal beneath was cold and unyielding, leeching warmth from my body as if it wanted to drain me completely. I didn't know how long we'd been locked in that cage below deck, as we'd had no sunlight to see by. Gone were the blue skies and white, wispy clouds, replaced by shadows, wood, and the smell of rot.

When we reached the city of Atlantis, I was hit with the pungent smell of waste and body odor. The paths were a combination of well-laid stones I'd later learned were called streets. Everything was new and bewildering and had names we'd never heard before, and we had no time to process any of it. The buildings rose in hard, straight lines, their dull monotony a lifeless imitation of the lush, untamed beauty of our island.

The soldier, Petros, presented us to the King and Queen without wasting any time. He swiftly told the King the details of Aella's strong fighting, Kassandra's meekness, and then of my bargaining and threats. When his report of their travels and our capture was done, the King and Queen walked up to our cage.

The King's gaze lingered on Aella, a strange, calculating glint in his otherwise pompous eyes, as he declared, "I'll keep the fighter for now. I want to see what she knows and if she can be trained."

"I have need of another servant. I'll take the golden one. My love, do you think it would be appropriate to gift the third to our loyal soldier?" The Queen batted her long lashes, her lips curving into the same honeyed smile I had seen Sirens use a thousand times before. But where my kind used it for survival, she wielded it like a blade, cutting down lives with a whisper.

"Your half-brother may have the girl," the King said dismissively as our fates were decided.

"You can't separate us," I protested as my sisters, and I crouched in our cage, holding onto one another.

"I am King; I can do whatever I want." He waved his hand, and more soldiers came to separate us.

Hands wrenched me away, my nails scraping against Kassandra's arm as I fought to hold on. Aella's screams rang in my ears, raw with fury. "No! Please—" My voice cracked, but the soldiers didn't care. My sisters were being stolen from me, and I was powerless to stop it. The soldier I'd been given to held me and made me watch as my sisters were taken toward the palace.

6

"I almost feel sad for you. After all, this is the last time you'll ever see either of them again," the soldier said as he held me tight to his chest despite my best efforts to break loose.

For ten long years, he held me against my will and forced himself on me nearly every night. For ten long years, I wished him dead, all the while hoping my sisters fared better.

Chapter 1

Recap: Kassie has been taken off into the swamp by Bigfoot, and Ella is injured but on the mend. Theia and Ella go into the swamp to search for their sister. You will find out what happened to Fin and Ella in Chapter 21.

Theia...

While Ella went one way to look for Kassie, I went another. It was a slight relief to be separated from Ella for a little while, but only because I knew I would see her again in a few hours. I was still furious at her for Kassie being gone, even though I knew it wasn't her fault. There was nothing that either of us could have done. If Bigfoot—no, Clay—hadn't come, Kassie would most likely be dead instead of simply missing.

The last two nights without Kassie had left me with flashbacks I didn't want. I tried not to think about Atlantis, but my body remembered even when my mind refused. The weight of chains. The cold press of a cage that was long since broken. And him—Petros.

Half-brother to the Queen of Atlantis. The first to shove my sisters and me into that cage as if we were animals. Beating me into submission, into unconsciousness, whenever I didn't please him and his wife. Callista hadn't been so cruel in the beginning, but when I grew pregnant the first time, her kindness turned to acid. In the decade I was forced to endure their abuse, she only conceived once, and she lost it early. To this day, I blame her for the loss of my first and second pregnancies.

I swallowed hard, shaking off the memories. Atlantis was dead to me; it should have been forgotten. So why did the shadows still whisper its name?

I trudged through the swamp, trying to focus. *Find Clay. Find Kassie. Forget the rest.* "Clay! Where are you?" I gritted out as I scanned my surroundings for any sign of them. There was no more hiding for him after the evidence we'd found on the boat. The fact that I'd pushed Kassie toward him made me even angrier. I was surprised Ella hadn't tossed that shit in my face yet. Then again, she wasn't like me. She might pick fights and be a bitch about most things, but low blows weren't her style at least not with us.

9

"Clay! Kassie! Where the hell are you?" I kept calling through the swamp, careful to keep an eye out for gators. I'd been at it for over four hours, trudging through the sucking pull of the soft ground, shoving and cutting through the thick foliage. When I caught up with that two-faced, shape-shifting boatman, I was going to tear him apart.

What pissed me off the most? I'd pushed Kassie toward him, told her to go scratch her itch, not knowing that he was fucking Bigfoot.

The stench of rotting eggs yanked me out of my anger, and my stomach clenched. Grunch.

They were nocturnal, which meant they were sleeping close by. Shit. If my weak nose could smell them, I was too close. I needed to get the hell out of Dodge before I woke them up. Ella and I could take them on together, but alone? I could handle one or two. More than that? I wasn't invincible.

I turned in slow, careful steps, scanning the swamp for any sign of the horrible creatures—and then the sound of wolves filled the air. The normal sounds of the swamp were shattered by the chorus of their howls, too close for me to run.

My pulse slammed into my throat.

My hands curled into fists as I readied myself for a fight I might not win—but I'd be damned if I went down easy.

10

***

Jackson...

The howling of my three companions and me filled my ears, a chorus of guttural growls as we caught the scent of the Siren—and something else. The air was thick with the stench of swamp water and decay, but it was the hint of blood orange that made my wolf's instincts snap into overdrive. The sweet, tangy scent poured into my nose, setting my feet pounding into the soft swamp floor, mud and moss squelching beneath my paws. Who was with the Siren that smelled so sweet?

The Grunch were nearby, but we had a singular mission. Rid the world of Sirens. We'd scented them in the area, but Grunch were nocturnal—nothing to worry about for now, as long as we didn't wander into their nests. I pushed forward, my pack and I charging through the underbrush. The air grew heavier, the intoxicating scent of hibiscus and blood orange pulling me forward like a lure. My wolf growled, sharp and possessive, driven by the scent of my mate... but fear gnawed at me too. Why would she be with a Siren, so close to the Grunch?

As we closed in on the Siren, I half-shifted back to my human form along with one of the others. This way, we could slash out the vocal cords of the Siren before she could entrap us. The other Lycan, who'd also half-shifted, was just feet ahead of

11

me as we entered the small clearing where the Siren was. His claws lashed out, tearing into the Siren's throat with a sickening sound, her vocal cords tumbling onto the swamp floor like twisted meat.

Pain and anger ripped through my very being at the sight of that female's blood spraying from her throat—*my female's* throat. Before I could attack my companion for harming my mate, three Grunch burst through the trees.

Leaning forward, I charged at the one closest to my mate and flipped it over my shoulder, letting it land on the soggy, moss-covered ground. My companions fought back, claws and teeth tearing into the nightmare creatures. But all I could see was her—her tiny body, limp and bloodied in the chaos. My wolf roared, demanding I protect her, and keep her safe.

I scooped up my female, her hands clawing at me even as consciousness faded from her eyes. Without another glance at the others, I ran back through the muck, my only thought, only instinct, to get my female to safety.

The sounds of the others quickly faded as I raced toward my Jeep. Just as I neared the edge of the bayou, I slowed down and looked at the female in my arms. She was tiny, her tattoos covered in blood and filth from the swamp. The faint, pungent scent of swamp water clung to my skin, mixing with the metallic tang of her blood. I could feel the wet heat of her body pressed against me—still, she was *too* still.

My mate was a Siren? *No.* My heart pounded in my chest with panic instead of adrenaline. Somehow, she'd entrapped me.

I shifted back fully into my human form and adjusted her limp body so I could open the passenger door and settle her in the seat. Reaching over her lifeless form, I grabbed my clothes from the driver's seat—jeans and a gray sleeveless shirt—and pulled them on before sliding into the driver's seat. "Fuck." I slammed my fist into the steering wheel.

I could feel the weight of the situation pressing down on me—the blood on my hands, the undeniable pull of my wolf toward her, and the gnawing fear of what this meant. She was a Siren, the enemy. My training had always told me to kill them. This shouldn't be happening; I was supposed to be the hunter, not the one falling for the prey. I couldn't go back to my pack, no matter my rank. I was a liability to them until I figured this out.

After taking a deep breath, I started the Jeep and pulled onto the road from where I'd been parked behind a large bush and some trees. There was a safehouse not too far from here that I would use. There were still around six hours of daylight left, and I had a blood-covered female in my passenger seat, so I would need to take back roads to get anywhere. My duffle was in the back

13

seat, though, and it had extra clothing in it, meaning I could put a clean shirt on the female now that she'd stopped bleeding.

My gut twisted at the memory of her blood spraying out as the other male had ripped out her vocal cords. This was what I'd trained my whole life for: hunting Sirens. My uncle had sent me on this hunt, my first hunt, because he'd said I was ready. Now their next in line had been entrapped by one of the very creatures our packs were meant to eradicate from existence. My uncle and father were going to be pissed when they found out, but I couldn't bring myself to kill the Siren, not when my wolf insisted she was *mine*, not when it insisted she was a fighter.

Pulling over again this close to my packmates was a risk, but driving around with my female looking the way she did was a greater one. My packmates were engaged in the fight with the Grunch, a fight I had no doubt they would win; they were evenly matched after all. I would face the consequences of getting my female to safety later. Pulling over not far from where I'd pulled onto the road, I rummaged through my duffle and pulled out two shirts. Swallowing hard, I looked at my female before wiping most of the blood with one and putting the other on her blood-covered body, arranging it in a way that hid her mutilated throat and the blood covering the front of her.

14

Pulling back onto the road, I punched in the address of a safehouse about an hour away. I couldn't shake the thought of what was at stake. Sirens were a threat to my kind—an abomination. Yet this one had tricked my wolf, convincing it that she was mine.

A little over an hour later, I pulled up to the safehouse. The drive on the bumpy back roads to reach it had felt nearly endless with the female in my passenger seat. My knuckles had remained white as I'd gripped the weathered steering wheel to keep from looking at her. Each glance at her left me with more tormented and conflicted thoughts. Though my shirt was clean on her, I could still see the blood, and her skin was pale and lifeless. But I shouldn't feel guilty or distraught for this situation. I should feel only the desire to remove her head from her body as my training demanded.

Our safehouses were hidden from human view, a necessity for shifting. An hour later, I stepped out of the Jeep, entered the passcode on the keypad, and left the door ajar as I made my way back to retrieve her. The sick, twisted feeling that gripped me when I lifted her limp body was nearly unbearable.

Once inside, I laid her on the futon, the standard in most of our safehouses, and cuffed her to the piece of furniture. I had no idea how long it would take for her to heal, but I knew she'd

15

need fresh clothes. I couldn't stand seeing her like this, bloodied and broken. As I thought about my own healing abilities, I knew I'd be safe to leave—knew she wouldn't regenerate before I returned.

As I left the safehouse to get her clothing, my mind kept racing. It would take me about thirty minutes to reach the store and find something suitable. I wasn't sure what size she wore, but she was tiny, so I'd go with a medium and something with an elastic waistband.

During the drive to the nearest supercenter, I made a decision—we'd stay at this safehouse until she regained consciousness. I'd deal with the consequences of leaving my packmates behind later.

Shame swept over me for abandoning them, but my wolf howled with fury that she was alone, and defenseless in the safehouse. I had to remind myself repeatedly. *She's a Siren. She's the enemy. You've been tricked.*

There were times when I felt like my wolf and I were separate beings, and this was one of them. My animal instincts had been fooled, but I knew what Sirens were capable of. They were dangerous to us, to everything we fought for. This situation was no different.

Chapter 2

Theia...

Pain radiated through my throat as I drifted back to consciousness. My vision blurred, but I could tell I was no longer outside. As the attack came rushing back, I jerked upright, my eyes widening when I saw my wrist cuffed to something.

A wave of dizziness washed over me. I pressed my free hand to my head, blinking hard to clear my vision.

"Once you calm down, I'll show you to the bathroom so you can get cleaned up and changed." A male voice drew my attention.

As my vision cleared, I saw him sitting in a chair not far from me, his presence sharp against the haze of confusion. He had dark, native skin with tribal tattoos on his face and neck. His dark hair hung in his face as he leaned forward on his knees and watched me like a predator.

17

"**I**'ve been dead… how much calmer do you want me to be?" My voice rasped painfully, barely more than a hoarse whisper. Each word felt like I was scraping glass against my throat. The male was holding something in his hands that I couldn't quite make out in the dim light. Why hadn't he turned on any lights?

"**Y**our head's still attached, so you weren't dead. If I uncuff you, are you going to attack me?"

Kassie, I'd been looking for Kassie. Fuck my luck. How was Ella handling all this? Now both sisters were missing, and I didn't even know for sure that Kassie was safe with that Swamp Ape.

Realizing I couldn't do anything about my sisters now, I shifted my focus to the male. "Dried blood itches," I muttered, my voice cracking from the effort. Talking felt like torture right now, but I couldn't resist. "You know, just in case you didn't notice." The scent of tonka bean and rich, sweet, smoky wood told me he was a Lycan—maybe even the one who had ripped my throat out in the first place.

Why wasn't I dead?

His jaw twitched as he stood and moved forward, using his thumb to unlock the cuff. Fucking biometric scanner bullshit. Then, before I could react, he'd fastened something around my

18

throat and put a hand over my mouth. "This is a shock collar. It is designed to keep Sirens silent."

A mother fucking bark collar? You had to be kidding me! I shot to my feet, and he didn't flinch, didn't back up even a step. The idiot probably thought I was as weak as a normal Siren. Shouldering past him, I looked around the room and spotted a bathroom through the open door behind the sleazy futon I'd been chained to.

I marched into the bathroom with the Lycan right behind me, practically breathing down my neck. Was the asshole really going to watch me clean up the blood he'd covered me in?

Looking down at myself, I realized I wasn't in just my clothes. A baggy t-shirt—one that smelled like tonka bean and exotic wood, and Gods, I hated that it actually smelled good—was thrown over my tank top. Great. Just what I needed.

I looked up at him with a "what-the-fuck" expression, catching him hovering in the doorway like some creepy guard dog.

"Humans couldn't see you covered in blood." His voice was casual, but there was tension in his jaw—clenching, unclenching. "There are clean clothes in the bathroom for you, and the collar is waterproof." He sniffed and cleared his throat, then shifted his weight to one booted foot. "I made sure it all had

19

elastic waistbands so it would fit since I didn't know what size you wore."

I blinked. *Wait... He bought me clothes?*

I opened my mouth, then closed it. No way. A Lycan had bought me clothes? Was I supposed to thank him now?

He caught my look and his eyes narrowed, like I'd just insulted him. "Don't look at me like that. I wasn't about to let a filthy Siren keep wearing my shirt. You didn't do a very good job of entrapping me. Now go clean yourself up and put on clothes that aren't caked in blood, or I'll fucking do it myself."

That's it. The asshole thought he was better than me? He actually had the nerve to put a fucking bark collar on me? Fuck him!

Without a second thought, my fist launched into his face, the satisfying impact sending him stumbling back a step. I slammed the door behind me and marched to the shower, but of course, the fucker had to follow.

Spinning around, I faced him with a twisted smile. Grabbing the hem of the shirt, I promptly ripped it up the middle to the neck and dropped it from my shoulders like a dirty jacket. My next act of rebellion was to flip him off with both hands.

He snarled. The next thing I knew, he was on me, grabbing my arms and slamming my back into the cold, unforgiving tiles. "Don't play with me, Siren."

I'd been here before. A slave. A possession. A body to be used and abused. But I wasn't that weak, mortal *child* Petros had tortured for a decade. "Bite me," I grated out against the shock that radiated through my throat, up into my skull, and down through my collarbone. My already damaged and healing vocal cords screamed in protest but I didn't care, it had been worth the pain to insult the fucker who thought he could control me.

"I warned you about the collar, now don't speak and you won't get shocked," he practically growled the words, still keeping me pinned to the wall. He looked me over and let go, stepping away from me. "Get cleaned up. We're staying the night here and moving on in the morning." With that, he left the bathroom, slamming the door shut behind him.

Self-hatred churned in my gut as the itch raged in me at the loss of his body heat. My fucking Siren side craved attention—demanded release and satisfaction. Too bad satisfaction was nothing more than a fleeting scratch against the surface of an endless pit of desire. No matter how good the sex was, the itch always came back.

21

Most of the time, it dulled to a hum—a constant lump in my throat, waiting. Being a Siren meant living with an unquenchable thirst, an ache that never truly faded. And it didn't give a damn that the male was a Lycan shit-bag. My body still craved his touch.

Stripping out of my blood and dirt-covered clothing, I stepped into the shower and wondered if I could get the fleabag in the other room to wash them so I could wear *my* clothes instead of whatever trash he'd gotten me. The thought of being dressed in shit provided by my captor left a bad taste in my mouth.

There was so much dried blood and dirt on me and in my hair that it took longer than I wanted to get clean. The water that ran off my body mixed in a dirty, sudsy swirl, funneling down the drain as leaves, twigs, and clumps of dirt caught on the metal lip. The filth of the swamp and my own blood had been caked under my nails, and I worked to scrub it away.

Getting out of the shower, I got water all over the bathroom because I had no idea where a towel was. Not that I gave two shits about soaking this dickhead's bathroom. Out of spite, I'd checked everywhere but under the sink for a towel.

When I finally dried off, I opened the bag of clothes he'd left on the counter: a shirt and women's jogging pants. No bra, no underwear. I rolled my eyes and put them on. Granted, he didn't know what size I wore, so I could let that slide—for now.

Marching out of the bathroom, a towel wrapped around my wet hair, I found the brooding pup sitting in a chair, staring daggers at the door. I put a hand on my hip and glared right back at him.

"Took you long enough."

I rolled my eyes in exasperation before pulling my bra out of the wad of clothing and holding it out, arching a brow. To my satisfaction, his face flushed.

"How was I supposed to know what to buy? Take yours off and check the tag?"

My eyes narrowed as I scrubbed my clothes together, then scanned the room. My gaze landed back on him pointedly. Surely, the dimwit would get that I was asking for a washing machine. I could go without a bra and panties, but if I had to run—which I fully intended to do—the support would be nice.

"I need to wash mine, too." He got to his feet and approached me. If I'd been a mortal, I might've shrank back, but I wasn't. I was a hellcat of a Siren. He looked me over, the flush of embarrassment gone. "You're almost completely healed. I didn't think Sirens healed that fast." He pointed to the left. "There's a

23

laundry room around the corner. Put your clothes in, then come sit on the futon."

Pursing my lips, I went toward the laundry room and loaded my clothes into the washer. After spotting the detergent, I started the machine. When I turned to head back to the living area, I almost collided with the Lycan. His scent hit me like a brick wall as he glared down at me.

"I told you I needed to wash mine too, so you just started it with only your clothing? Typical fucking Siren—only thinking about yourself."

My brows shot up, and I pointed to the collar around my throat, then flipped him off and gave him a big-ass smile. This dog could go fuck himself. He snarled, his body brushing dangerously close to mine as he shoved past to stop the washing machine. I didn't flinch, but damn, my heart kicked up anyway. As he pushed by me again, he marched into the living area. I followed him loosely, then veered off into the kitchen to see what food and alcohol I could find.

"What the fuck are you doing?" he snapped as I opened the fridge.

Smiling to myself, I grabbed a beer and popped the top as I shut the door. The can hissed open, the sharp scent of beer mixing with the still-tingling rush of anger running through me.

24

Without breaking eye contact, I tipped the can back and took the first drink to fuel my tolerance for his bullshit. He couldn't expect me to answer with a fucking bark collar on, could he?

A low growl rumbled in his chest before he turned and marched into the laundry area, looking at me over his shoulder like I was actually going to try to make a run for it. Sure, I was reckless, but I wasn't stupid. I wasn't about to try to bolt with this collar on. Not yet. I'd wait for the right moment. I wanted my own clothes when I left this shit-head anyway.

"Didn't I tell you to sit down?" the dog snapped at me, but I pointedly ignored him as I leaned against the counter, enjoying my beer.

He sighed, clearly fed up, as he opened the fridge and grabbed a beer. Leaning against the other counter, his gaze locked with mine. "You're supposed to be dead right now, you know that? My pack hunts and kills your kind for the shit you do."

I rolled my eyes and kept drinking. I might as well be as annoyingly *silent* as possible. I set the beer down, put my hands on either side of my head, and tugged upward before shrugging. *Still attached.*

"No shit. You fucking entrapped me."

Picking up my beer and crossing my ankles, I shook my head in the negative. I'd not hummed a single fucking tune. I'd

25

been taken by a crazy pup. *I wonder if he's rabid.* I just continued to stare at him. Fucker wanted to take me captive then I was going to make it awkward as fuck.

"What was a Siren doing in the middle of the swamp anyway?" His eyes narrowed, refusing to break eye contact.

"Pole," zap "dancing." The second zap was worth the look on his face. The way this dog turned red was priceless.

"It was a rhetorical question! You knew you were going to get fucking shocked!"

That's why he turned red? He was mad that I'd shocked myself? *Interesting.* That led to the question of why I wasn't dead. Chewing on my lip ring, I glanced around the space and noted no trace of anyone else. Hadn't there been more than one of them?

"Don't worry, no one else is here." He pushed away from the counter and opened the freezer. "I grabbed a frozen pizza. As far as I know, you need to eat too." I watched him put the pizza in the oven, then start rummaging through the cabinets. This must be some sort of safehouse. A few minutes later, he set a pizza cutter down on the counter and grabbed a couple of plates. Why was it always pizza?

I tipped my beer back and finished it off before moving to the fridge to grab another one. What I wanted was a bottle of

26

tequila, but I wasn't about to beg this fucking mutt for it. If I was going to be stuck here with him, I might as well make him work for it.

"Do you prefer something other than beer?" he asked, pulling me from my thoughts. It wasn't like he even cared, but yes, dog boy, I wanted something else. So I nodded.

"Looks like you're shit out of luck tonight," he said, his voice low and rough. "Maybe if you're not too much of a pain in my ass, I'll let you go to the store with me tomorrow to get something else... and some more clothes. Ones that fit you better." He rubbed the back of his neck. "I guess I should've figured you'd be a small or some shit. I mean, you're fucking tiny."

He walked up next to me and opened the fridge to get another beer for himself. He let it shut and looked down at me. "It's all part of the Siren bait; looking all delicate and sweet, even being physically weaker than other immortals. But you're a fucking monster, aren't you? Just waiting to entrap a male to do your little fucked up Siren bidding."

Excuse the fuck out of me?

I was about to hit him when he chuckled and leaned down closer to me. His scent filled my nostrils as I heard him breathe in my scent in exchange. "I wonder if that's why you smell so good, because you're a Siren." He was so close that I could feel the heat

27

emanating from his body. He put a hand on the fridge behind my head, making me realize that I'd ended up with my back practically against it.

"Strange to think something so pretty can be so terrible." He stepped away from me then. "I'll figure out what to do with you later. Tonight, let's just eat and get some rest. You did just have your throat ripped out this afternoon." Like I could fucking forget.

We ate the pizza in silence once it came out of the oven. I was good at ignoring tension, but it looked like it was eating away at the dog, the small vein in his neck pulsing and giving him away. Good. Fucker should just let me get back to looking for Kassie. Not that I was about to tell him about my sisters. Was that why I was alive? Had they heard me calling for Kassie, and he was now planning on using me to get to my sister somehow?

The wolf got up from the table, rubbing the back of his neck, then went back to the kitchen, where he opened a couple of drawers again before finally pulling out a notebook and a pen. "What were you doing in that swamp, anyway?" He shoved the notebook at me, and I arched a brow. His jaw clenched. "How about a different question—do I need to be concerned that one of your victims is lost in that swamp?"

Smiling at him, I took the paper and wrote, *I don't leave victims alive. Wanna be my next?*

"Are you crazy? Like, actually mentally unstable?" He stepped up to me, crowding my personal space, and I just looked up at him with my shit-eating grin. "You are a tiny, weak, immortal who's been cut off from her powers, and you want to threaten me?"

Shoving him out of the way, I wrote more on the paper. *Why am I alive?* I looked at him expectantly.

"You entrapped me. If I kill you, I'll go mad."

Shaking my head, I wrote, *Nope. You're just too much of a pussy to kill me. My name is Theia, by the way. I think I'll name you Scruffy.*

"Goddess, you really are nuts." He rubbed his forehead.

The shit I've lived through? Yes. I'm unhinged. I'd like to go back to my swamp now.

"You're not going back to your swamp."

What are you going to do with me then? Be a good boy, Scruffy, speak.

He slammed his fist on the counter. "My name is Jackson, and I'm keeping you until I figure out what else to fucking do with you."

Could I help myself? Yes. Did I want to? No. So I wrote back, *Bad dog, no barking at me.*

The next thing I knew, he yanked the pen out of my hand and threw it across the room, making me let out a small giggle—which earned me a healthy zap from the collar. Flipping him off, I shoved him out of the way, which wasn't easy since the fucker was huge, and opened the fridge to grab another beer.

He slapped his hand on the door before I could pull it open. "What the fuck is wrong with you? Do you even give a shit about your situation?"

With a huff, I elbowed him in the ribs, making him double over and let go of the fridge. Calmly, I opened it, grabbed a beer, and walked to the futon—the only place that looked like it might be my bed.

It wasn't that I was giving up. I just didn't have an escape plan yet. No clue where I was. No idea if I could overpower the Lycan or get his thumbprint to unlock the collar. Ella and Kassie would have to be okay without me for a little while.

Jackson stomped his way around the counter to where I sat drinking my beer in the dimly lit space. "Try that again, and you'll regret it," he warned. Before I could react, he snapped a cuff around my wrist so fast I hadn't even seen it coming.

30

Letting out a gust of breath, I yanked on the cuff. This was going to make things difficult. I'd hoped he'd think I wasn't enough of a threat to lock up, but apparently, I'd gone too far. Shrugging, I decided I'd just drink my beer and try to get some rest while I plotted my escape from the dog.

<u>Chapter 3</u>

Theia...

Sleep never fucking came to me. Why would it? Kassie was missing, and Ella was alone. This dumb dog thought he was making the world a safer place by silencing one more Siren when, in reality, he'd left possibly the most dangerous Siren to ever exist unchecked. Ella was dangerously unhinged. There was little doubt in my mind that Kassie and I were the only reasons she hadn't destroyed the world, one haunting melody at a time.

Filtered sunlight coming through the blinds told me it was morning. Sitting up as best I could, I looked over at the sofa where the Lycan had decided to sleep. The fucker wasn't moving yet, so I started yanking on my cuffs to cause a clinking sound, hoping it would wake him. He opened his eyes and glared at me after only a couple of yanks on the cuffs.

32

"I suppose you want something."

In response, I pointed to the bathroom and raised a brow. Sighing, he got up and used his thumbprint to unlock my handcuff.

"Your clothes are clean and in there, but they're a little ripped up. You may want to keep wearing the ones I got you for now."

Rolling my eyes, I shouldered by him and into the bathroom. I didn't give a flying fuck if my clothes were torn up; I wasn't about to keep wearing the shit he'd gotten me unless I had no other options. Shutting the door on a snarling Lycan, I changed into my own clothes and emptied my bladder. Splashing water on my face after washing my hands, I walked back out of the bathroom, leaving the clothes he'd bought on the floor.

"I bought a frozen breakfast bowl for you. You can eat it or go hungry until lunch." He glared at me from the kitchen where he stood with his arms crossed in front of the microwave. Rolling my eyes again, I walked into the kitchen and opened the freezer to get out the frozen trash he'd decided was sufficient. Going to the microwave, I flopped it on the counter next to him and crossed my arms, giving him an expectant look. Fucking take me hostage. Stupid shithead.

33

His hand shot out and locked around my throat, jerking me to him. His face was inches from mine. "You've got some fucking nerve for a Siren without her power."

"Food-dog," I gritted out through the shock of the collar and smiled as the electric pulse zapped his hand, making him release me.

"Fucking fix it yourself." He yanked open the microwave, pulled his food out, and walked away. The itch screamed at the loss of his nearness, my treacherous nipples hard and aching from how dangerously close he'd been. "As soon as you're done, we're leaving. It's not safe for us to stay here after yesterday."

Taking a steadying breath, I put my food in the microwave and moved on with my morning. It was going to be a long fucking day.

***

Jackson...

We reached the second safehouse, and the stale air of the small, dimly lit space hit me immediately. The walls were bare, the floors creaked underfoot with every step, and a sense of suffocating quiet seemed to press in on me as soon as we crossed the threshold. I managed to get her inside without too much of a struggle, handcuffing her to the futon in the corner. The sound of the cold metal clicking into place felt louder than it should have,

34

like it echoed off the empty walls. Her glare was ice, but that wasn't anything unexpected.

I left her there to glare at me as I walked to the kitchen, pulling out a pad and pen. I'd spent most of the day in a daze, trying to figure out who I could trust enough to call. A Siren, a fucking Siren. The weight of the decision sat heavy in my chest—had I done the right thing? I saved her life. But the more I thought about it, the worse it got. If anyone found out, I'd be a traitor, a liability. My pack would never trust me again. And I'd just abandoned the wolves I'd left behind to save her—who could I turn to now? The idea of keeping her alive, even under these circumstances, gnawed at me. I couldn't seem to shake the feeling that I was in way over my head. My pack couldn't trust me. The proof of that was the wolves I'd left behind when I'd saved her.

Pulling out my cell phone, I began dialing numbers. My thumb hovered over the contacts on my phone for a second longer than necessary before I dialed the number. I could feel my pulse hammering in my ears, the cold sweat on the back of my neck reminding me that there was no turning back now. I needed help.

Great moon Goddess, I'd saved the life of a fucking Siren. I was in deep shit. "I need a list of Witches, Wizards, Warlocks, Sorcerers, and Priestesses—the more powerful, the better," I said as the call connected on the Lycan helpline. Most immortals used

35

a few of the same organizations, but Lycans had their own trusted networks. Not just Lycans, but most of the immortal Shifters out there used a separate set of organizations. We had trust issues, especially when there were deadly females out there hell-bent on destroying the sacred bonds between mates. We had to take extra precautions.

"I've sent you the list of trusted contacts," came the distorted voice on the other end. Always taking precautions, I couldn't even tell if I was talking to a male or female.

"Thank you for your assistance," I said before hanging up the phone and checking my text messages.

I stared at the long list of names, each one blurring into the next as my mind scrambled. Two hours. Two fucking hours of calls that led nowhere. It felt like I was running in circles, no matter how fast I moved. I couldn't get the image of Theia out of my mind—her stubborn eyes, her defiance. I wanted to be angry with her, to stay in control, but it was getting harder with every passing second. And then there was the matter of her fucking *song*. No one knew what it would take to break me from the Call, but the more I thought about it, the more I realized I was running out of time—and options.

Finally, I reached someone who said they could help me as soon as they answered the phone, without me even having to speak a word. "You don't even know why I'm calling."

"Don't underestimate me, Lycan, you have a Siren who makes your wolf drool, and you are looking for a severing spell. I'm not just a master of spells and potions, I'm a seer. You will need a fresh sheet of paper and a pen so that you can write down the list I'm about to provide you," the voice of the Priestess was young but full of authority. It wasn't surprising that her voice was young; most immortals stopped aging around twenty-five or so.

"I'm ready, or had you already seen that?" I questioned with sarcasm dripping from my tone as I put her on speaker and set the phone on the counter.

"You know well, seers do not see everything. You will need the following items in order for me to assist you. I will meet you in Washington State. I'll contact you later with the address you will need. You will need to get Gorgon scales, Centaur hooves, hibiscus pollen, crushed black lotus flower, three vials of weeping water, Phoenix feathers, two black candles made from an Ogre's ear wax, and thread."

"Where the fuck am I supposed to get all of this," I growled as I finished taking down her ridiculous list.

37

"You are a smart pup with plenty of resources; you will find all of this in due time. I'll text you anything I feel you need to know. Tell the Siren: Bigfoot is careful with his flowers. If you'll excuse me, I have other calls that will be coming in," she said just before the line went dead as she hung up on me. I gritted my teeth and glared at the phone. This was ridiculous! What other option did I have, though? I could either get the items this female wanted or be bound to a fucking Siren.

I looked back at the list, the weight of it sinking in like a boulder in my stomach. What the hell was I supposed to do with all of this? It felt like the universe had conspired to throw every rare, dangerous item at me in a single breath. I'd take care of the easier things first—hibiscus pollen and the black lotus flower were obtainable. But Gorgon scales? Centaur hooves? That shit was impossible. And yet, there I was—staring at the possibility of being bound to a Siren for the rest of my days.

"What the fuck did she mean Bigfoot is careful with his flowers?" I muttered as I looked toward the Siren. She had her eyes closed and was leaning her head back on the futon. It wasn't like the Siren could talk to me anyway, not with the collar on. Sighing heavily, I ripped the page from the notebook, folded it, and put it in my wallet. Next, I tore another sheet of paper from

38

the pad and set the pen down as well. I wasn't about to give her the whole notebook to fill with stupid dog insults.

"I'm going to uncuff you so you can write some responses to questions. You get one fucking sheet of paper. Don't waste it," I warned as I walked over to her and used my thumb to release the cuff.

She rolled her eyes and went to the counter where I had the paper and pen. I watched as she picked up the pen and began to write. *I want to go to the store and pick out food for dinner. Frozen pizza is stupid.*

"How is that supposed to work?" I demanded, crossing my arms and glaring at the tiny female.

We get in the car, drive to the store, and buy food. I know how to cook, dickhead.

"I didn't say you couldn't cook. You are my captive; therefore, I can't just take you to the supermarket and parade you around in handcuffs."

Where would I go? IDK where I am and need your thumb to get the collar off.

I read her scribbled response and thought for a moment while I looked at her.

39

You can always put a leash on my collar and tell people I like kinks and am mute if it makes you feel better. I can't keep eating frozen trash when my cooking is better. Hell, you tell me what you want, and I'll make it.

"Are you into kinks?" The question came out before I could stop myself.

Bad dog. Talk food, not foreplay.

Tensing my jaw in frustration, I reined myself in. I couldn't get mad at her for snapping back in the only way she could when I'd just asked what I had. Hell, part of me respected her refusal to surrender easily.

"Fine. I'll take you with me to the store, but you stay right with me. And just so you know, if anyone tries to remove that collar without my thumbprint, it will liberate your head from your shoulders."

Who am I going to run into in the store? I'm exhausted. Can we just go to the store so I can make real food? And pick out my own clothing? You have horrible taste.

I had a feeling my jaw was going to hurt from biting back my anger with her constantly. "Are you trying to push me to end you?"

I was minding my own business in the swamp, and you ripped out my throat and fed me frozen trash. How am I supposed to act?

"Like a fucking captive instead of a bossy mute."

Her lips curved upward at my response, and she went to write something else on the paper, but I pulled it away from her. "We're done here."

She chewed on her lip ring, and Goddess save me, it took everything in me not to grab her and bite that damn lip myself. *Fuck I want her.*

Then she flipped me off and gave me that look that said she didn't give a fuck how dangerous I was. She was infuriating and sexy as hell all at the same time. Snarling, I stepped away from her.

Chapter 4

Theia...

The fact that we were actually in a store was a little shocking to me. I'd honestly expected the Lycan to put up more of a fight or flat-out ignore me, yet here we were. Not that I had a whole lot of freedom as we walked through the store with his arm wrapped around my waist. To the mortals shopping, we looked like a happy couple. They had no clue he was holding me captive.

As we walked through the produce section, a woman with a septum piercing and a spiked dog collar around her neck stopped and looked me up and down. "Cool collar, where'd you get it?"

"I gave it to her," Jackson said quickly.

She scoffed and looked him up and down. "I wasn't asking you. Women can have a voice too, you know."

Oh, I like her.

42

"She's mute." Jackson's tone was flat, but his hand tensed on my waist.

Rolling my eyes, I decided to sign to the girl, whether she'd understand me or not, I didn't care. I knew ASL and was going to play the part and insult the mutt, even if he didn't know it. *'Don't mind him, he's been living off frozen trash. Once I feed him real food, I'm sure he'll be a good boy and let me rub his belly.'*

He glared at me and signed back, *'I didn't catch all of that, but I know it was rude. Watch yourself.'* His hand movements had been jerky, an indication of his agitation with me, even if there had been a brief moment of surprise.

Quirking a brow, I signed more to him: *'Careful with the foreplay, she might understand.'*

"This was weird," the female said, knotting her brow as she grabbed a bell pepper and left.

'I like her.' I signed and smirked at Jackson, knowing he had not.

"You would," he shot back in a disgusted tone. "Get what you need for whatever it is you want to cook, so that we can get out of here."

'Afraid to be seen with me? You could always just take the collar back and let me go. Pretend this never happened.'

43

"Goddess, there's not going to be any shutting you up now," he grumbled.

'Worth a try. Just follow me like a good puppy and I'll get what we need for real pizza.'

He shifted closer to me and growled his response in my ear. His growl sent delighted tingling across my skin. "I'm far from a puppy, Siren; watch yourself."

I turned, angling so that I was facing him, and raked my eyes over his face, feeling heat between my legs at the way his voice had sounded in my ear. I'd be damned if I would let him or the itch control me. *'Be a good dog and fetch me tomatoes.'* I signed.

"Pick out your own damn tomatoes," he snapped. He stepped away from me, pinning me with a glare. He knew I wouldn't run, not when I had no idea how to remove the collar without blowing my head off. I winked at him and started shopping with a little more freedom. Pissing him off to the point he didn't want to touch me had been easier than I'd thought.

I filled the cart with tomatoes, olives, oregano, parsley, spinach, mozzarella, garlic, pepperoni, sausage, olive oil, flour, salt, pepper, and baking powder. As an afterthought, I added a half-dozen eggs, sugar, and powdered creamer to the cart. I

44

wasn't sure how long we'd stay at the current safehouse, so buying milk didn't seem like the best idea.

"Satisfied?" he asked as I frowned at the cart.

'I need some more clothes, just one or two changes should do if I can wash them. And tequila or vodka, it's better than beer.'

"I wasn't planning on making you wear dirty clothes," he muttered as he grabbed the cart and pulled it toward the clothing section of the supercenter. Once in the clothing section, I grabbed a couple of dark t-shirts with skulls and shit on them and two pairs of jeans. Then I tossed a black lace bra and a couple of black thongs in the cart, partly to fuck with him, and partly because I did need underwear. To my disappointment, he didn't seem to care about the undergarments.

He'd stopped by a liquor store on the way back to the safehouse. He'd gotten a bottle of vodka and a twelve-pack of beer. When we got back to the safehouse, I didn't waste any time getting started on making the pizza. I was about to teach this dog the difference between frozen trash and proper nourishment.

"I'm surprised you know sign language," he said as I began mixing the flour, a tablespoon of baking powder, and a teaspoon of salt with my hands.

'I could say the same about you. What made you learn?'

45

He took a drink of his beer before answering. "One branch of my pack began deafening all the male offspring to protect them from your kind a few decades back. It created a need to learn for the rest of us who'd not been mutilated in the name of safety."

I stopped and just stared at him, not sure if he was serious at first. *'WTF, that's horrible! Just because they might one day encounter a bad Siren?'*

"All Sirens are bad. Look at you. I'm not sure what your fucking playing at, but I don't trust you. Why do you think I'm watching you cook?" He scowled at me like all the wrong done to those males was *my* fault.

I rolled my eyes. *'You bought everything that's going into this; what am I going to do? Smother you with the raw dough?'*

"The fact that you thought of something says a lot." I narrowed my eyes at him, then tossed some flour in his face. "What the hell?"

Giving him a tight smile, I flipped him off and turned to rummage through the cabinets to get a bowl or cup to mix the oil and water in after setting the oven to 425. I filled a large coffee mug with about a cup of water. Then I added around a tablespoon of olive oil and mixed it with a fork. Once they were whisked, I

46

began adding them to the flour mix until I was able to work it into a shaggy ball. *Fuck.* I'd forgotten to dust the counter with flour.

Looking at the male who was watching me, I nodded at the bag of flour. *'Sprinkle some flour out for me.'*

"You're the one that's supposed to be the cook here," he reached over and did as I'd asked anyway. Rolling my eyes, I flopped the dough out and began to knead it until it was smooth. While I allowed it to rest for about five minutes, I cleaned my hands and moved on to preparing the vegetables and cooking the sausage.

I put the sausage in the pan, the sizzle rising up as it hit the hot surface, releasing an earthy, savory scent that filled the air. I chopped it up with a spatula, the sound of the meat breaking apart sharp and satisfying. The lid went on, trapping the heat and smell, while I turned my attention to the remaining ingredients. The faint crackle of the sausage simmering in the background contrasted with the silence between us, the only sound in the kitchen aside from the occasional clink of the knife on the cutting board.

'Watch and learn, pup.' I signed, my hands quick as I put the large head of garlic on the counter and cut the top off. Pulling out foil, I set the whole thing in a makeshift bowl and drizzled it

47

with olive oil, salt, and pepper. Next, I pinched the foil closed around it, put it on a pan, and stuck it in the oven.

'Half an hour and it will be ready.'

He snorted and took another drink of his beer. The male was a fucking dickhead. Narrowing my eyes, I picked up the tomato and began slicing it, placing the slices on a plate. Blinking, I looked at the knife in my hand.

"I'd break your wrist before you could use it. Just go back to playing chef," he said, as if reading my mind. I wasn't thinking about using it on him; I was just surprised he'd even risked it. Then again, he had no idea I wasn't as weak as a mortal like other Sirens. Shaking my head, I went back to chopping the ingredients I'd gotten for the pizza. Once that was done, I pressed the dough flat on a pizza pan and brushed it with a little more olive oil.

Layering the sliced tomatoes, sliced mozzarella, and olives over the pizza, I wondered what my sisters were eating tonight. Kassie could cook, but Ella hated anything domestic. Were they together? Shaking my head to dislodge the thoughts, I sprinkled the spinach over it and dotted it with pepperoni. Turning to the stove, I stirred the sausage.

While it finished cooking, I grabbed the vodka I'd stashed in the freezer and splashed some into the first cup I found. I put the bottle back in the freezer; it wasn't exactly cold yet, but I

48

didn't care. I needed the burn of the alcohol to help with the damned itch in my throat.

It was too easy for my mind to conjure the fantasy of that dickhead tossing me on the countertop and fucking me senseless while he kneaded my breasts the way I'd kneaded the dough. I wanted him to fuck me with the aggression I could feel radiating from his body. I wanted to drag my nails over his skin and make him fucking bleed while I orgasmed. Yeah, I needed the vodka.

"Fuck," he said as he stood up and walked away from the counter to flop on the futon in the living room. He could smell my arousal. I took another drink of the vodka and focused on the food, hoping I could push down the need to tolerable, non-daydream levels. I turned back to the sausage and finished cooking it, then tossed it on top of the pizza.

The wait for the garlic to finish cooking was annoying, to say the least. While Jackson glared at me from the living room area, I busied myself cleaning up the mess I'd made. The task didn't distract me much from the thoughts of my sisters.

Had I been home with Kassie and Ella, Kassie would have been in the kitchen helping me while Ella sharpened a knife or played with her switchblade at the table. Maybe. The itch had been driving us to isolation recently. The need to have our desires

49

met left us all on edge and ready for a fight or a fuck. I could use a good fight right now to take the edge off.

The oven timer went off, pulling me out of my thoughts. I pulled out the garlic, squeezed it out onto the pizza, and put the pizza in the oven for the next fifteen minutes. The smell was mouth-watering as I pulled it from the oven and set it on top of the stove. Jackson came trotting into the kitchen, a dog led by his nose. I cut the pizza and set a plate in front of him with a triumphant smile.

He cast a suspicious gaze at me before taking a bite. The groan that escaped him was so purely masculine that a new wave of lust washed over me. *Motherfucking itch!* I forced myself to think about anything else. The fight with the Grunch recently was a good distraction. They smelled horrible! Closing my eyes and leaning back against the refrigerator, I remembered cleaning up the mess of bodies on the lawn. That did the trick. It also made me less hungry.

Opening my eyes, I noticed Jackson watching me carefully. Shaking my head, I grabbed a slice of pizza, the vodka from the freezer, and sank to the floor. It would be easier if I didn't have to *see* him. Being a Siren meant that males turned me on even if I hated them. Males had taken everything from me all those millennia ago. Males had separated and tortured my sisters and me. We'd fixed that, though. Those males were nameless and faceless in history, forgotten by everyone.

"At least if you're eating it too, I know it's not poisoned." Jackson's voice sounded from the other side of the counter. Leave it to him to pull me out of my thoughts; not that I was complaining.

Shoving to my feet, I set the bottle down on the counter and tilted my head as I looked at him. *'I'm going to sleep, you annoy me.'*

"I annoy you? Seriously? You have been calling me names and insulting me non-stop." His labret piercing was catching in the light at this angle and nearly distracted me from what he'd said.

'Poison is boring.' I signed with a dismissive flick of my hand.

"So I'm *annoying* because I don't trust you? You're a Siren, you can't be trusted by nature. You entrap males to do your bidding."

Rolling my eyes, I flipped him off and walked to the bathroom. I was done with the conversation. Thanks to not sleeping the night before, I was exhausted and just wanted to shower and sleep. I ignored his grumbled comments and shut the

51

door to take my shower in peace. I was sure that when I got out, he'd cuff me to the futon again. Jackass.

***

I'd been right. When I'd gotten out of my shower, my moody guard dog was waiting with the cuffs in hand. Snatching the cuffs out of his hand, I put one around my wrist and marched to the futon without looking back at him. It wasn't like I could make a run for it with the explosive bark collar around my throat. Lying down, I cuffed myself to the damn futon, pulled the blanket draped over the back over me, and stared at my palm, letting myself wallow in the fact that I was alone again for the first time since Atlantis.

Chapter 5

Theia...

Picking up my child, I cradled him to my chest, casting one last look at the body of his father before slipping into the streets. I had to get out of the city. If I had reached my immortality, then my sisters would have as well, and I could only pray that fate would reunite us one day.

Theo let out a strangled cry.

My breath hitched, my vision blurring as I looked down. A spear jutted from his tiny back, his small hands trembling as they clung to my robes. Blood bubbled from his lips. His wide, tear-filled eyes met mine, pleading—confused—hurting.

"Theo," I gasped, my voice breaking and my own pain forgotten.

I pressed my shaking hand to his face, brushing his tears away as the light in his eyes flickered. His fingers twitched against me, and his body sagged.

No-no-no!

A raw, guttural sob ripped from my throat as I pulled him closer, rocking him as if I could will life back into his little body. Power and anguish filled the sound like nothing before.

Footsteps approached.

The soldier who had impaled us knelt beside me, his voice eerily calm. "How may I please you?"

The world blurred, my vision tunneled. My heartbeat was a deafening drum in my ears as my shaking hand closed Theo's dull eyes. Hot tears scaled my face as my heart shattered over and over again with each beat in my chest.

I swallowed, my throat tingling, power thrumming beneath my grief. I looked down at Theo's peaceful face, placed a trembling kiss on his forehead, and whispered, "I will never leave you."

"Remove your spear," I said in a shaking voice. Around me, shadows shifted—men stepping out of their homes, drawn to me like moths to flame.

He obeyed instantly, yanking the weapon from our bodies. My own wound meant nothing. The pain was hollow, eclipsed by the gaping void inside me.

I stood, still cradling my son, and embraced the strange tingle in my throat, the anguished power burning there.

The first note was a whisper of sorrow. It carried on the air like a funeral wail, curling through the streets, sinking into the ears of every man who heard it. I sang as I walked, stepping over cobblestones slick with blood, my voice swelling with grief and fury.

Around me, men stopped what they were doing, their movements jerky, their eyes blank as they turned to follow. Women screamed. Mothers yanked their children inside, slamming doors.

I wasn't alone for long. Two more voices rose in harmony—one filled with rage, the other with chilling detachment. Kassandra. Aella.

We emerged at the entrance of Atlantis together, our song a spell, a curse, a reckoning.

I turned to the soldier who had killed my child. My voice was calm and steady. "Take your knife and slit your throat at my feet."

He did. Blood gurgled from his throat as he collapsed. It wasn't enough. It would never be enough.

"Set fire to the city," Kassandra commanded.

Aella's voice was ice. *"Fight to the death."*

"All of you, slit your throats," I commanded, my voice steady despite the searing pain lacing through me.

The ensnared men obeyed without hesitation, steel biting into their own flesh as blood pooled at their feet. Women screamed, clutching their children as they fled from their homes. Some tried to pull their husbands and fathers back from the edge of death, but the men remained unmoved, bound by my voice, lost to my will.

"The women should take their children and leave this city." My tone was cold, hollow, my grief a weight that threatened to crush me. I tightened my arms around Theo's lifeless body, my vision blurring at the edges. Pain radiated through every fiber of my being—mind, body, and soul fracturing under the weight of loss.

"This city will pay for what it's taken from us," Kassandra murmured, her voice thick with sorrow. She turned toward me, her gaze flickering to my son, devastation etched into her face. *"Most of all, what it's taken from you."*

I looked down at Theo, pressing a trembling kiss to his forehead before turning my back on the city. I didn't need to watch the carnage unfold—the sound of flesh splitting, of fire crackling, of men screaming in blind devotion was enough. The scent of burning wood and charred bodies filled the air.

I walked forward, stepping through the sea of fleeing women and children, and sank to the ground against the towering cliff wall that bordered the road leading away from Atlantis. Kassandra and Aella followed, wordlessly sitting beside me. The terrified survivors kept their distance, giving us a wide berth as they passed.

And then silence.

The only sounds that remained were the distant crackling of fire and the eternal, rhythmic whisper of the ocean against the shore.

At some point, one of my sisters had packed my wound, staunching the bleeding as I cradled Theo's body and wept. I didn't know how much time had passed, only that my world had shrunk to the weight of my son in my arms, the soft strands of his hair beneath my fingers. Struggling to hold onto consciousness, unable to bear the thought of looking away from him.

I don't know how long we sat there, I only know that eventually, the only sounds were those of the fire destroying the city and the ocean on the other side of the cliff wall. Aella had joined Kassandra in resting her head on my shoulder, both sisters *giving me what comfort they could. Then water washed up over my toes until we were sitting in gentle, ankle-deep waves.*

We looked up to see Poseidon standing before us.

The Sea God gazed down with a sorrowful expression, the shifting tide swirling around his feet. His presence was undeniable, ancient, and vast; a force as eternal as the waves themselves. We had seen him only once before, long ago, as our mother had hidden us away.

"I have been searching for you, my Sirens." His voice was low, reverberating through the air like the pull of the tide. "This is not what I expected to find when I heard your call."

I swallowed, my throat raw with grief. My fingers tightened around Theo's small form. "Can you give him back to me?" My voice cracked on the words, my desperation bleeding through.

Poseidon stepped forward and extended his arms. "Give me the child."

A sob threatened to choke me. I pressed one final kiss to Theo's forehead, his skin cool beneath my lips. "I love you," I whispered.

Then, with shaking hands, I placed my son into the arms of the Sea God.

58

Poseidon cradled him with surprising gentleness. Lifting his trident, he met my gaze. "Place your hand on his chest."

I obeyed, pressing my trembling palm against Theo's tiny body.

"I cannot heal his flesh," Poseidon murmured, his voice thick with something that sounded almost like regret. "But I can return him to you."

The trident glowed, burning with golden light. A sharp, searing pain exploded in my palm. I gasped, yanking my hand back, but Theo's body—his soft, tiny frame—was gone.

Vanished.

"No!" My cry tore from my throat, raw and broken. I staggered back, my head whipping around, searching, clawing at the space where he had been. "What did you do to him?"

Poseidon remained unmoved. "Look at your palm."

With shaking fingers, I turned my hand over.

A mark had been burned into my flesh; a seahorse, delicate yet unyielding, forever etched into my skin.

"He's a part of you now," Poseidon said. "It was too late to heal his body, but his soul will never pass through the Underworld. He will remain with you, wherever you go."

The weight of his words crushed me. I dropped to my knees, fresh tears slipping down my cheeks. My son, my baby...

"He didn't deserve to die," I whispered, voice barely audible over the distant roar of flames.

Poseidon turned toward the smoldering ruins of Atlantis. "Leave now, my grandchildren, for this city shall never rise from these ashes." His expression hardened, and the waves surged at his feet, swallowing the shore, reaching hungrily toward the crumbling walls. "I will bury it beneath the waves and sands of the sea."

His gaze darkened, and for a fleeting moment, I saw something dangerous flicker in his depths. "As for your mother... she will be dealt with for keeping you from me."

Then, like foam dissolving into the tide, Poseidon vanished into the waves.

And Atlantis began to sink.

Jackson...

I woke to the distressed sounds of my female and the sharp zapping of the shock collar as she cried out a male's name. My stomach twisted.

Bolting upright, I found her glaring at me, one hand clutching her throat.

"I hate you," she choked out, her voice garbled and broken by the collar's relentless shocks. Tears streamed down her face, and I felt something inside me crack.

60

"Stop talking," I ordered, intending to remove the collar.

"Go to hell!" she practically screamed. "I hate you! I hate you! I hate you!" She thrashed, fighting my advance with her one free hand, the other yanking against the cuffs.

I didn't know what else to do. She was hurting herself, the collar shocking her repeatedly. My mind scrambled for a way to stop her, to silence her—so I did the only thing I could think of.

I kissed her.

Her body stiffened in shock. Then, unbalanced, she fell backward, dragging me down with her. The zap of the collar seared through my lips, but I didn't care. I shoved my hand between us, pressing my thumb to the release mechanism at her throat.

The collar clicked open, and I should have pulled away. But then her fingers slid into my hair, her body arched up into mine, her lips moved against mine. A groan rumbled in my chest before—

She jerked away.

"No!"

Her hands slammed into my chest, and before I could react, she kicked me off her. Hard.

I hit the floor, pain lancing through my ribs as the impact drove the breath from my lungs.

"What the hell?!" I rasped, pushing myself upright.

My words died in my throat.

She was clawing at her own neck.

Before I could move, before I could stop her, she dug her fingers into her throat—

And ripped out her own voice box.

Blood spilled down her chest, thick and dark. Her mouth opened like she was screaming, but no sound came out. Only tears, only the sheer agony on her face as she collapsed back onto the couch, her body jerking as her life drained away.

For a second, I couldn't move.

My brain refused to process what I'd just seen.

Then, instinct kicked in.

I lunged forward, fumbling with the cuffs, my hands shaking too damn much. The moment they unlocked, I scooped her up and carried her into the bathroom, barely aware of my own ragged breathing, and of the blood soaking into my clothes.

She just—she fucking—ripped her own throat out.

I gently set her down in the tub.

Then, I sat on the toilet, gripping my thighs so hard my nails threatened to break skin.

And I waited.

Waited for her to regenerate.

Waited for her to wake up.

Waited for answers, because I didn't know what the hell had just happened.

But when she came to, she was damn well going to explain.

Theia...

"Who the fuck is Theo?" Jackson growled as I came too, my eyes blinking against the harsh light.

Everything hurt, especially my throat. I lifted my head and looked around in confusion. "Am I in a bathtub?" I asked, my voice rough. Speaking was not easy after regenerating my vocal cords. Especially with the way I'd ripped them out.

"Don't play games with me, Siren. Who is Theo?" He demanded.

Pain filled my chest, and I closed my eyes tight against the tears that I wouldn't shed in front of him, not again. "Why does it matter?" I countered in my broken voice.

"Did you think I was him when you pushed up against me? Were you lost in a little Siren fantasy of a lover from your past?" he demanded in a condescending tone. He leaned closer as I looked away from him. "Did it make you mad that I was the one kissing you and not him? Your precious Theo?"

63

I twisted around and slapped him across the face. "Don't ever, *ever*, say his name again." Tears began to slip from my eyes, my pain and anger mixing in a way I couldn't control.

His hand was wrapped around my throat before I'd finished my sentence. His grip was tight, his jaw twitching as I gave him an order he probably wouldn't follow. He leaned in next to my ear and did the worst possible thing; he said my son's name.

Rage filled me as I twisted and tried to pry his hand from my throat. "I'll kill you, I'll fucking kill you," I said in my choked and distorted voice. My weakened, healing body left me feeling like a mortal.

"Not before I hunt down this, Theo, and kill him," he threatened.

"He's already dead," I yelled at him. My silent tears turned into sobs as I relived his death all over again. The Lycan pulled back his hand as if I'd shocked him. Glaring up at him, I fought to get my crying under control. I shot out my hand, palm exposed. "Here's Theo, here's the reason I hate males, here's the innocent *baby* that was killed because he was unfortunate enough to have *me* as his mother!"

He stood and took a few steps back. "Baby? Theo was your son?"

64

I turned away from him, wiping the snot from my nose. "Did you think we were infertile?"

"I thought Sirens only birthed daughters," he said in a stupid voice.

"Unless something has changed in 12,000 years, my sisters and I are capable of having either gender." It was my turn to use a condescending tone, still refusing to look at him.

"I'm sorry," he said in a quiet voice as he knelt beside the tub again. Suddenly, the collar was back around my neck.

"I hate you," I said through the zapping of the collar. It struck me that they must have done experimentation to find out if the collars would work or not, and I had a new hatred for him and his kind.

"Sirens are a plague on this Earth, entrancing and destroying males with their songs. Did you really think telling me of your loss would make me willing to let you cast your spell on me?" he asked, his eyes haunted, and his expression hard.

'Go away,' I signed. I didn't want him around while I grieved. I was a captive, again, just like I had been with Petros and Callista. The husband and wife duo that had tormented me for ten long years.

"I'll bring you clean clothes, and you can wash the blood off. Then we need to leave."

65

I didn't watch him leave the room; I just pulled the curtain and let the hot tears spill down my face as I lay in the tub. I didn't bother standing up and stripping my ruined clothing until I'd heard him deliver clean ones.

My shower; that's how long I would allow myself this little pity party. Twelve thousand years ago, I'd been mortal, possessing the physical strength of a human and little to no knowledge of the world. It was likely that I was older than Jackson, and with that age, came the advantage of knowledge and patience. My only true master, however, was the damn itch.

Chapter 6

Jackson...

Guilt gnawed at me as I listened to the shower turn on. She'd lost a child because of what she was. In all my years of training, all the times I'd been told of the plague that were Sirens, I'd never once considered their children. How many mothers had my kind killed? Was it possible for a Siren to be male? I'd never heard of it. She said she had sisters. Was it because all Sirens are female? All we knew was that they could only reproduce with immortals. That's why they entrapped our kind.

-PING-

My phone buzzed on the counter, pulling me out of my thoughts. I picked it up, swiped to unlock the screen, and read the text:

One thing I forgot to tell you about the black lotus—it needs to be the immortal

67

black lotus. I'll send you an address.
There's only one place in this realm to get
it. Lola will be expecting you.

With a heavy sigh, I set my phone down and pulled out the eggs the Siren had grabbed yesterday. While she showered, I made omelets. Was this my way of apologizing to her? Sirens entrapped males, destroying their minds and the mate bond. I shouldn't feel bad for her—shouldn't feel bad for any of them. Was this Siren different somehow? Was she really my mate? No. That was her cursed magic trying to work on me.

If she were truly my mate, the Priestess wouldn't be helping me. She'd known what I was calling about and had the spell needed to sever the bond of the Siren's Call. How she'd managed to entrap me was a question I'd mulled over many times. None of the Lycans I'd been hunting with had hesitated. I still couldn't remember hearing her sing. When a Siren entrapped you, did you remember hearing their song? Had I not been howling loud enough?

The bathroom door opened, and she walked out, her damp hair hanging around her, blue highlighted strands brushed back from her face. She didn't look at me, her eyes avoiding mine as she moved to the couch. Her posture was stiff, guarded, like she was trying to shut me out—and somehow, it worked. Pain

68

tightened my chest, and I clenched my teeth. Grabbing a plated omelet, I took it to her with a fork. "There's coffee if you want some." With that, I went back to the kitchen and began cleaning up in silence.

Theia...

Jackson had been quiet since I'd gotten out of the shower. When the dog had handed me an omelet, I'd been a little shocked. We were now in his Jeep, driving down a Texas highway. He'd told me we were going to see an Elf. The quicker we got the ingredients, the quicker I would be rid of him and he of me.

The question was, when he was able to sever the bond he felt, would he end my existence or let me go? Everything he'd said indicated that he wanted to kill me, but the attraction he felt to me was stopping him. Was I actually his mate, or was it just guilt twisting his emotions?

I should have some sense of self-preservation, but as I looked at the seahorse in my palm, it was hard to find the will to keep going. For so long, my sisters had been my reason for living, but they weren't here. Could they continue without me? If I were to die, would I be reunited with Theo? I closed my hand into a fist, casting my gaze out the window before tears could betray me.

69

Before I knew it, we'd reached a restaurant and bar called Lola's. "Time to talk to the Elf. Just behave in here so we can get this done with and move on." Jackson's voice was tired and distant, reflecting how I felt—empty, lost, and uncertain.

We walked inside, and he turned right, guiding me by the elbow as though I would run. What could I do? If I were 'rescued' by a mortal, they wouldn't be able to get the collar off me.

We reached the bar, where a heavy male was polishing glasses. Inhaling, I caught his scent—something like engine oil, whiskey, and leather. Goblin.

"I was told Lola would be expecting us," Jackson said, his voice tight as his hand slipped onto my lower back.

In front of mortals, we had a part to play. His touch shouldn't mean anything to me, especially when I was pissed and hurting, but the itch didn't care. His hand on my elbow had been enough to start the constriction in my throat. But his hand on my lower back... that was enough to have my entire body waking up with need.

The Goblin's eyes flickered to me and lingered just a moment, noting the collar on my throat before snapping back to Jackson. Was he going to help me? His nostrils flared, and his eyes returned to me again. Fuck. My scent had cost me what could have been my rescue. Whether he smelled my arousal or

70

scented me as a Siren, he wasn't going to help. He pointed to a door and lifted the bartop for us to walk through.

"She's moody for an Elf," he warned in a low voice. "You and that female should tread lightly."

Jackson turned and locked eyes with the Goblin, his jaw ticking as he clenched and unclenched it. "*My* female and I are none of your concern, so keep your eyes and nose to yourself, Goblin."

Whoa. Had he really just called me his female? Fuck. That. Jerking away from him, I shoved open the door to the back room, which looked like a stockroom.

"Damn it, Theia, what the hell?" Jackson demanded as he followed me through the door, shutting it behind us. Jackson's voice was tight with anger as he snapped, "I told you to fucking behave, and instead, you act like a damn brat." There was a long pause as the words hung in the air. I could feel the weight of his gaze on me, pressing in like a storm on the horizon, but I refused to meet it. The silence stretched longer, suffocating, before I finally flipped him off, earning an angry growl from him.

"What do you want?" A female voice demanded from an office to the left.

Ignoring Jackson, I moved toward that door, where I was met with the sweet scent of black currant and jasmine.

71

"I've come to get the immortal black lotus," Jackson said from beside me, just as the female stepped out from behind a desk.

The curvy female who stood there, arms crossed and looking us over, wasn't what I'd expected from an Elf. The majority of the elves I'd encountered in my lifetime were tall and typically very thin. This one was around five-foot-five, with full curves, pouty lips, and a warm, golden-brown complexion. She had shoulder-length dark hair and amber eyes; her scent was the only thing typical of elves.

"Who told you to come to me for black lotus?" she demanded. I immediately respected her for not being intimidated by the Lycan at my side.

"A Priestess and Seer. The female doesn't offer room for negotiation." Jackson's tone was curt and to the point.

The Elf frowned and pulled the chain around her neck, lifting a vial filled with black dust. "My mother gave this to me when I was a child, in case I was indeed an Elf. It was so that I could one day return to Lufkin.

"You are an Elf, and Lufkin is a few hours from here. Are you going to give it to me or not?" Jackson snapped, seeming to always be in a bad mood.

"She was a human, and Lufkin is in another realm, Lycan. It is the Elven city of Aetheris," the Elf stated in a bland tone before walking to a shelf and pulling out a Ziploc bag. "I'm not giving you all of it. As my mother was mortal, this is all I have left of her." I watched as she carefully opened the small vial on her necklace and tapped a portion of its contents into the Ziploc. "This should be enough. With this flower, a little goes a long way." Closing the bag, she shoved it at Jackson with a peeved expression. "Now, if you don't mind, I have a business to run."

"What do I owe you for it?" Jackson asked, agitation seeping from him.

"Anonymity. Don't tell another fucking soul where you got this. If I find out my name has left your mouth, you'll regret it."

"I don't fucking plan on it," he grumbled, shooting a glance at me.

'Who would I even tell?' I signed incredulously. *The nerve of him!*

"Didn't I tell you two to leave? You can have your little silent conversation back at the bar or something."

I didn't wait for Jackson. I just turned on my heel and left. There was no conversation to be had—silent or otherwise. I was his fucking captive, just like I'd been someone else's all those

73

years ago. I marched past the Goblin and out the door, headed for the Jeep. I didn't know where I was, except that I was probably still in Texas. I had no phone, no transportation, and no voice, unless I wanted a painful shock.

Jackson was hot on my heels, though, as if I would fucking run with nowhere to go. Getting into the Jeep, I slammed the door shut and buckled up, silently waiting for my captor to take us to his next destination. A destination I had no say in, but one that was important to my future, one way or another.

"What the fuck was that?" he demanded as he got into the driver's seat, slamming his door hard enough to shake the Jeep. I blinked at him and gave him a bland look. I wasn't in the damn mood. "You need to fucking stay with me!" Jackson's voice was harsh, but I could see the strain in his eyes. But there was something else, too. Something between the lines of his words, a flicker of something... protective? The idea caught me off guard. "Did you see the way that Goblin reacted when he caught your scent? Don't you get it? You're a fucking Siren, you are in danger from every male who figures out what you are. You can't just hum your little fucking tune and turn them into your slave anymore! Fuck. Just, don't pull that shit again."

With that, he started the Jeep, and we pulled out of the parking lot.

74

Chapter 7

Theia...

Jackson's words had left me shocked, confused, and enraged. I didn't turn males into my slaves! Not that I could fucking tell him that thanks to the damn shock collar around my throat. It was a constant reminder of just how little control I had, but I wasn't as defenseless as he thought. Not that I wanted him to know that just yet. I still hadn't figured out how I was going to escape—not when the fucking collar posed the problem it did.

After leaving Lola's, we went to a supercenter where Jackson grabbed string from the crafting section and some small jars. To my surprise, he led me to the grocery side and told me to figure out something for dinner. His silent presence loomed close to me, doing little to cool the heat building in my body. I was simultaneously pissed at him and attracted to him, the confusion stirring a tangle of emotions inside me.

Once I'd filled the cart with what I needed—which wasn't much, considering it was just the two of us—I signed to him that I was done. But instead of leading me to the front like I expected, he guided me toward the garden center. Once we were there, he started browsing the flowers, and I fought the urge to roll my eyes. Then he came up to a stand with hibiscus flowers and plucked one, holding it out to me.

"Come here, I want to put this behind your ear," he said, a smile tugging at his lips.

Why? I signed, confused and a little wary.

He stepped closer, brushing my hair behind my ear with surprising tenderness, his smile widening. "Because we're on camera, and I need the pollen. This way, it looks like I'm flirting. I don't want to buy the whole damn plant."

I raised an eyebrow and smiled back, giving him my most sultry look before signing: *I hate hibiscus. Put it in your own hair.* I didn't need to tell him how the flowers were the last thing I'd seen on that island before we were stuffed into a cage and forced into slavery. The thought twisted in my chest like a knife.

His eyes flickered, and his smile faltered for a moment before he stepped even closer. His fingers brushed against my skin as he tucked my hair behind my ear again, his touch

76

lingering just a fraction too long. "Just until we get to the Jeep, brat."

The way he said *brat*—and the feel of his fingers grazing my skin—sent a shock of heat through me. It made me want to go weak in the knees, but I wasn't about to let him win this little game.

I touched the flower delicately, letting it fall slightly to the side, then faked a bashful smile. Standing on my tiptoes, I kissed him lightly on the cheek. The shock on his face was priceless, and for a moment, I allowed myself to revel in it.

I want to do terrible things to you. I signed, my fingers moving with deliberate slowness. He could take it however he wanted because I meant it on so many levels.

"Don't do that again," Jackson's voice held an edge I hadn't heard yet. Had I gone too far? Or not far enough?

I chewed on my lip ring, looking him over, savoring the way his posture shifted—just a subtle change, like I'd unsettled him. *Good.* He deserved to feel uncomfortable. I nodded toward the checkout and turned away from him, satisfied with the power I'd just wielded.

No sooner had we gotten to the Jeep than he ripped the flower from behind my ear and stuffed it into one of the jars he'd grabbed. We loaded the bags into the back, and the drive to the

77

safehouse was about thirty minutes. The entire way was quiet, and unlike this morning, the silence between us was thick with tension.

When we finally arrived, I brushed by him, making my way straight to the kitchen without a second glance. It was my fault he was in a mood, and I was more than a little pleased with myself. The idea that I'd gotten under his skin was... powerful.

Setting aside my thoughts of Jackson, I tossed the ground chicken into a skillet and turned on the burner. As the meat cooked, I sliced a zucchini in half lengthwise, cutting off the stems. I used a spoon to hollow out all four halves, tossing the extra into a bowl for a side dish. I rubbed the zucchini down with oil, salt, and pepper, then slid it into the oven to pre-cook for a few minutes.

Once the meat was cooked through, I added cilantro, diced jalapenos, feta cheese, and sliced tomatoes, stuffing the zucchini boats I'd made. I slid them back into the oven and turned my attention to the zucchini 'guts' I'd set aside. Adding olives, more tomatoes, and mushrooms, I tossed the mixture into a skillet with olive oil, salt, pepper, and fresh garlic, letting it fry. The kitchen filled with the savory aroma, its comforting scent eased the tension in my shoulders and calmed my mind.

"Fuck, that smells good. Do you always cook like this?" Jackson's voice interrupted my focus as he stepped into the kitchen, grabbing a beer from the fridge.

I stepped away from the stove, my eyes sweeping over his face, lingering on his lips. Lips I wanted to kiss. *'I like things that taste good,'* I signed, then opened the fridge and pulled out the tequila he'd bought me the night before.

"Then it's a good thing I bought a good bottle of that shit."

"Yep," I replied, and felt the sharp jolt of shock course through me.

He glared at me. "What the hell? Did you fucking forget you can't talk?"

Shrugging, I flipped him off before turning back to the stove. I set the tequila bottle down beside me and stirred the vegetables in the skillet. I hadn't forgotten. The silence was getting old. Pain was part of living. Every damn day was painful for me. Not the same as Ella or Kassie—each of us had our own demons.

"Fucking Sirens," Jackson muttered, turning to leave the kitchen.

I glanced around, then grabbed the lid of the tequila bottle and hurled it at him, hitting him right in the back of the head.

79

"What the fuck!" He spun around, clearly pissed.

"Ass," I choked out, not giving a damn about the shock that followed.

"Stop talking!" he snapped.

"Or," I taunted, feeling the shock pulse through me again, "what?" I set the spatula down, crossed my arms, and locked eyes with him.

"I'm warning you, stop talking." He edged closer to me, his nostrils flaring with agitation.

"Make me," I challenged, pushing through the shock just enough to get both words out.

He shoved me back into the cabinets of the L-shaped kitchen, his hands planting on the countertop on either side of me, his body towering over mine, trapping me in. "Shut your fucking mouth before I shut it for you, brat."

My lips parted as I looked up at him, but then I shoved him away, going back to cooking. I had to ignore the electric pull of my body toward his.

He snarled, storming out of the kitchen, snatching his beer as he went. He tried to sit at the table without glaring, but his body was stiff with tension. I smirked, a rush of satisfaction flooding me. I'd gotten under his skin just as much as he had with me.

80

When the food was ready, I plated everything and sat at the table with my meal, leaving him to serve himself. He sat down across from me, and I watched his reaction, as I had so many times in my old life. If the food had been unsatisfactory, it would have been thrown on the floor, and I would have been punished for wasting it.

He held my gaze as he took his last bite. "The way you're watching me, I'd almost wonder if you poisoned me—but I bought everything in it." He tossed my own words from last night back in my face.

Setting my fork down, I wiped a small bit of food off my lip and slowly sucked it off my thumb. I savored the sensation, letting my eyes linger on him, watching as his gaze darkened and his nostrils flared slightly at the subtle challenge. Then I signed: *Just wondering if you actually like my cooking, or if you eat anything, like any other dog.*

His palm slammed onto the table with a sharp crack, making the dishes jump; the force of it rattled through the room. Had I not been baiting him, his reaction would've made me jump. "I'm not a fucking dog. I'm a Lycan."

"Same thing," I choked out, fighting against the shock collar.

81

"Stop that!" He shot to his feet, bracing himself on the table with both hands, practically snarling at me.

Giving him a sassy look, I toyed with my lip ring before shooting back, "Bad dog—" zap, "No barking."

He rounded the table to where I was, and I got to my feet, ready to meet his challenge. "Stop fucking talking!"

"No." The one word was more than enough to push him and was utterly worth the pain. In truth, part of me was hoping the repeated assault to my vocal cords would help soothe the itch. I was getting desperate, just like Ella.

What I hadn't expected was for his lips to crash against mine. One hand locked on the back of my head while his other arm banded around me, pinning me to him. He sucked my lip ring into his mouth for a moment before breaking the kiss that had my whole body fucking burning. "I told you to stop before I made you, and I meant it."

As quickly as he'd grabbed me, he stepped away. "I'm getting a shower," he practically snarled as he walked over to his bag and pulled out the familiar handcuffs. "Come sit over here, you can watch TV or something."

Crossing my arms over my chest, I glared at him. I'd given him no indication that I was going to try to escape. "You have two choices: You can walk to the futon and sit your bratty little ass down, or I'll pack you over there myself."

Picking up the bottle of tequila off the table, I slowly and deliberately brought it to my lips. Without breaking eye contact with him, I took a long drink, savoring the burn as it slid down my throat. I didn't move—wouldn't move.

"Fine, have it your way." His voice dropped into a dangerous growl. He prowled toward me, his every step predatory, his gaze fixed, unwavering. The air between us felt charged, like something was about to snap.

I held my ground, but beneath my bravado, my heart thudded in my chest. Did the fucker actually have the balls to follow through with his threat?

<u>Chapter 8</u>

Theia...

It hadn't been a threat. The fucker had tossed me over his shoulder and chained me to the couch before taking his damn shower. When he'd come out, he was wearing nothing but a pair of low-slung sleep pants, his dark hair damp. I raked my gaze over him without a hint of shame. The male was fucking eye candy—lean muscles, tattoos, and piercings everywhere.

He unchained me, then ordered me to take a shower, telling me to 'wash the brat off,' as he put it. I didn't argue. It was the only time I had to myself, so I made the most of it.

Afterward, Jackson had commanded lights out. He settled into the bed while leaving the door open, his gaze fixed on the futon where I was chained to sleep. He could see me from where he lay—always watching, waiting.

I shifted on the futon as much as I could, but the pulsing ache between my legs kept me wide awake. Clawing out my

84

vocal cords hadn't even taken care of the damn itch for a full day. If I were home, I'd try to take the edge off by masturbating, but that wasn't an option here.

I opened my eyes to glare at my captor, who I thought would be asleep, only to find him sitting on the edge of the bed, scowling at me from the bedroom. "What?" I snapped, earning a painful shock to my vocal cords. The jolt radiated up into my jaw and ears for a few seconds.

He growled at my pain. I rolled my eyes and flipped him off before rolling onto my side and closing my eyes. But suddenly, his weight pressed down on top of me, rolling me to my back. His arms braced on either side of my head, and his legs straddled mine.

"I can fucking smell you," he breathed into my ear, his voice thick with something dangerously close to hunger. I pressed my hand against his chest while yanking once against the handcuff that shackled me to the futon. "You act like you want to push me away, but it's a game, isn't it?"

"Get off," I gritted out through the shock of the collar, half pushing with my free hand.

"You'd like that, wouldn't you?" he taunted, not budging as he lay on top of me. "For me to get off. You filthy Siren." The

85

way he said filthy Siren didn't sound like an insult but a compliment.

His body pressed into mine, the heat of him radiating through me. I could smell him too—his masculine, woodsy scent enveloped me, making my mind go dizzy for a moment. The ache between my legs flared at his touch—at the way he made my body betray me.

He growled, and I could feel the twitch of his erection through his thin pants. My body acted against my mind, my hips arching up into him. "Fuck," he cursed and surged off of me. "You haven't entrapped me enough to do your bidding just yet, brat."

"Not"—zap—"entrapped," I grated out, welcoming the slight pain to my vocal cords.

"Why else would I crave you this way? Why else would a Siren smell like my mate?" he demanded.

Did he expect me to answer? Every time I spoke, I got shocked, thanks to the Siren bark collar he'd put on me. Then the grumpy asshole would get pissed because I'd hurt myself.

"Leave me alone," the words came out distorted, but clear enough for him to understand.

Another low growl rumbled from him, and my treacherous body reacted to it. My mind wondered what it would feel like to

86

have him growl between my thighs. "Are you in fucking heat?" He was next to me again, one hand braced on the arm of the futon as he leaned over me, his chest heaving as he breathed in my scent and glared at me.

"Go to hell."

"Stop that! You could just nod your fucking head yes or no! Or fucking sign! Why do you have to speak?"

With a defiant lift of my chin, I responded, "To piss you off."

He growled and crushed his lips to mine. His body was over me again, his heat seeping into mine, bringing my already heated body to a new level of hot and bothered. He broke the kiss and cupped my cheek. "Is it to piss me off, or do you just want to make me kiss you?"

I glared at him, breathing through my nose for a moment before responding, "Fuck you."

He growled again and moved his hand from my cheek to my breast, causing me to suck in a sharp gasp and arch into him again. "Am I to take that as a yes?"

"Go to hell," I gritted out, my heart pounding in my chest, my core throbbing with desire, my breasts tingling with anticipation. I fucking wanted him. I wanted him buried inside me, kissing me, fucking me, devouring me.

87

He slid his hand down to my crotch, and I wanted to twist away from him. I really did. But my body arched into his hand instead. His breath was hot against my ear. "You want me to touch you, don't you, brat?"

"Yes," I gasped out against the zap of the collar, unable to deny what I knew he could smell.

"You want me to fuck you senseless, don't you?" he breathed in my ear, his hand rubbing against the apex of my thighs, his restraint unraveling.

"No," I choked out, fighting both the collar's sting and my own need. I wasn't about to give in entirely to this male.

"Liar," he murmured, his lips brushing my skin as his hand moved back to my breast. "I can smell how much you want me, feel how hot your body is. You want me."

"Touch only," I managed, each word a battle against the collar's punishing jolt. If he could give me release without taking me, I wasn't going to pass it up—not when the ache was so unbearable I wasn't sure I could contain my power.

He growled against my neck, his breath hot between the collar and my ear. "Fucking brat."

His hand slid down, fingers teasing at my waistband. Then he lifted his head, pinning me with a sharp glare. "If I touch you—if I ease this fucking need—will you shut up?"

88

I glared back, hating him, wanting him, craving him. My jaw twitched as I clenched my teeth. What other choice did I have?

"Fine."

He growled again and slipped his hand into my pants, his fingers thrusting inside me.

"Fuck, you're wet," he muttered, his voice rough with need.

My head fell back, hips tilting up as he pumped his fingers in and out of me. The sensation coiled tight in my core, heat surging through my veins. A moan escaped my lips, and the collar punished me instantly, a sharp jolt tearing through my body.

He snarled, pulling his hand from me. "That won't do. I can't make you cry out in pleasure if you've got this damn thing on," he said, his thumb tracing the collar's edge. "But I can't take it off you, can I?"

"Make it worth the pain," I bit out between shocks, my hand fisting in his hair as I yanked his lips to mine.

He groaned against my mouth and shoved his hand back into my pants. "Challenge accepted," he growled, teeth tugging at my lip ring.

His lips crushed against mine, his tongue thrusting deep, mirroring the relentless rhythm of his fingers. It was a battle—every stroke, every movement a test of will. Would he push me over the edge, or could I hold on? He sucked my lip ring into his mouth, nipping at it, pulling just to the point of pain before trailing his lips down my jawline, leaving a path of heat in his wake.

My hips rolled with his touch, desperate for more. I craved his weight on top of me, the solid press of his body pinning me down, branding me with his heat until he was burned into my very marrow.

The tension built, winding impossibly tight, my body trembling on the edge. Another moan tore from me, the collar shocking me mid-sound. The pain twisted with the pleasure, pushing me higher, making me reckless.

"Stay with me, brat," he ordered, voice dark and commanding. "I want you to know whose fucking fingers you're coming on. Open your goddamn eyes."

My lashes fluttered, my vision locking onto his golden gaze. And just like that, I shattered.

A silent scream wrenched from my chest, my body convulsing around him as wave after wave of release crashed through me. Jackson held my gaze, fingers driving into me until I had nothing left to give. My limbs went lax, my breath ragged as I lay there, spent and panting.

"Good girl," he murmured, pressing a kiss to my cheek, just beside my ear. "Now get some sleep. We have a lot of ground to cover tomorrow."

Then he was gone, slipping off the futon and heading for the bathroom without another word.

I lay there, staring at the ceiling, my body still humming with aftershocks.

What the hell had I just done?

Chapter 9

Theia...

The next morning, the scent of brewing coffee greeted me, and I woke to find my wrist uncuffed. Strange, considering Jackson had so little trust in me. Shuffling toward the bathroom, I wondered if it had anything to do with what had happened between us last night.

When I reentered the main space, I found him staring at me from the kitchen. Nope. He still didn't trust me.

Wordlessly, I moved to the coffee pot, pouring myself a cup before adding my usual milk and sugar. That sugar added to the coffee was probably the only sweet thing about me. The thought almost made me smile.

"Let's see if you're a brat of your word," Jackson mused, watching me from the corner of his eye as he leaned against the counter. "I'm curious if you can actually keep that pretty little mouth shut."

92

I huffed, setting my cup down before signing, *'Don't start barking at me before I've had my coffee. I'm not a morning person.'*

"You're a brat is what you are," he muttered before taking a sip of his coffee and looking away.

I had expected some awkwardness after last night, but instead, he was still the same insufferable jackass. How was it that a simple kiss on the cheek in a store had thrown him off, but last night hadn't fazed him at all? Had I imagined it? If he hadn't just thrown our 'deal' in my face, I might've questioned whether it even happened.

Sipping my scalding cup of heaven, I closed my eyes and thought for a moment. Nope, his comfort wasn't working for me.

Setting my cup back down, I reached over and tapped his shoulder. When he looked at me, I signed, *'One orgasm. One day.'*

His nostrils flared, his expression hardening, but I caught the hint of pink trying to creep into his cheeks. "Don't toy with me, brat."

Shrugging, I picked up my coffee and made my way to the futon, sitting cross-legged with my eyes closed. Last night had been unexpected, but not unpleasant. In fact, I needed to stop thinking about it, because I already wanted a repeat.

93

Then again, orgasms were hard to come by.

Not that it was grounds for another round.

I'd be escaping soon enough—then I could find someone else to scratch the itch; someone who wasn't holding me captive.

The biggest obstacle to my escape was the collar. The cuffs, I could work around—I could cut off my hands and slip them free. It would hurt like hell, but they'd grow back, and faster if I kept them and let them knit themselves back on after.

Damn. I really wasn't looking forward to that.

Still, I'd try to get out of all the restraints first and then bolt.

"You should eat something. We need to get moving soon. I don't like sitting still for long."

Frowning, I looked at him. *'Why?'*

"Not that it's any of your business, but my uncle's pack will be looking for us. They want you dead. I've been paying cash for everything so they can't track us yet, but eventually, that's going to run out, and I'll have to use a pack credit card."

'Why not just kill me?'

I probably shouldn't have asked that, but a small part of me wanted this never-ending sorrow to end. And for that to happen, my life had to end.

94

Jackson's expression darkened, resentment filling his voice as he glared at me from the kitchen. "You fucking entrapped me, remember? I can't kill you, or I'll go mad."

Right. He still believed that.

How the hell was I supposed to prove I hadn't entrapped him? I didn't want to be mated to a damn dog who despised me. I didn't want to be mated at all. I lived only for my sisters.

Setting my coffee down, I signed, *How do we fix that? I don't want to be tied to you either.* It wasn't like he knew I'd overheard his conversation with the Priestess as I'd been pretending to sleep.

A flicker of shock crossed his face before he quickly masked it. "We're getting the ingredients for a severing spell. Once it's done, I'll no longer be entrapped to you."

'Then you kill me.' It wasn't a question.

Lycans have been attempting to eradicate Sirens for approximately the last 150 years. His jaw ticked, but he remained silent.

I would face my death without flinching. My only regret would be not saying goodbye to my sisters.

'So, what's next on the list for this spell?'

"If you think I'm going to kill you, how do you expect me to trust you to help?"

95

I shrugged. *'I'm over 12,000. If I die, I die. Maybe gathering the ingredients will be fun before I go.'*

He shook his head. "I don't know what I'm going to do with you. Not right now. You're a Siren—a threat to any male who can hear you. If I let you go after all this, who's to say you won't entrap another male? It's in your nature."

'So kill me. But grant me one last request before you do. Deal?'

"What if I just leave that collar on you? Then you get to live, and no one else gets entrapped."

He was looking at me like he actually meant it. Like, he was seriously considering keeping me collared forever. He couldn't be, not when he kept reminding me how awful Sirens were.

"Fuck it. We'll cross that bridge when we come to it," he muttered. "Finish your coffee, and we'll head out. We forgot to grab anything for breakfast, and I'm hungry." He took a slow sip of his own coffee.

Without hesitation, I signed, *'I've got something you can eat.'*

He choked, coughing hard, and I laughed—only for the shock collar to cut me off with a jolt of pain.

Totally worth it.

96

'Worth it.' I signed with a huge grin.

"Fucking brat." But there was the ghost of a smile and a chuckle—his first since we'd met four days ago. And Gods, did that quick little dimple do things.

Nope. Not going there. Not again.

Last night had been enough. But fuck, what his mouth had felt like on mine...

I was losing my damn mind.

"Anyway," he said, clearing his throat, "when you finish your coffee, we'll go get something to eat. It's gonna be fast food, so don't get excited."

Excited. Hot. Bothered. Too late.

I was all of those things for the fucking prick who had kidnapped me.

The idea of spiking my coffee with tequila was starting to sound real appealing.

Shouldn't I be *less* wound up after last night?

Hell, he'd actually given me an orgasm with just his fucking fingers.

***

Theia...

We'd just reached a fast-food joint and ordered some

breakfast sandwiches when Jackson's phone pinged. He led me to a table before bothering to read it. I had to wonder if it was his pack trying to find out where he was, since he'd said they might be an issue. Little did he know, my sister was probably a much bigger issue.

We sat in the plastic booth, tucked away from the few others there for the morning. As I looked around, I speculated that most people were eating on the go instead of dining in. At least the white laminate tabletop was clean, even if the place smelled like old grease. Then again, most fast food places did.

I wondered if Ella had found Kassie as I unwrapped my breakfast from its white paper. Had she heard the wolves? How could she not have? Had the other wolves gotten her? No, I wouldn't let myself go there. If the other wolves had encountered Ella, they were dead. Sure, I could fight, but Ella was a fucking badass. She thrived on learning every fighting style possible. There was a reason neither Kassie nor I had been able to beat her in a fight in centuries.

Surely, Ella had found Kassie by now. She'd want her help to track me down. My situation was so fucked. I wasn't afraid of death, but how would my sisters handle it? Did they really need me? It was partially my fault Kassie had ended up getting taken by Clay in the first place. Had I not pushed Kassie into the relationship, Ella wouldn't have been so recklessly pissed.

"You good over there?" Jackson's voice broke into my thoughts. I looked up at him to find him staring at me, mild concern on his face.

'What was the text about?' If he wanted to ask questions, fine; I'd ask my own. I wasn't about to tell him about my sisters. I would die to keep them safe.

His eyes narrowed slightly, and a small crease appeared on his forehead as he hesitated. Then, he glanced around before answering in a low voice. "The Priestess sent me a location to get the next item on the list. We have a destination."

Looking down at my hands on the table, I felt the weight of his words pressing on me. Each item we checked off the list was one step closer to breaking the bond between us and allowing him to kill me. The hum of the neon lights suddenly felt louder, the clink of kitchen equipment echoing through the establishment.

'How long until we get there?' I signed and looked back up at him.

He looked away from me, apparently not willing to make eye contact. "It's a couple of states away, so a few hours still. Depending on what we come across on the way, we'll get there today or tomorrow." Thanks to our conversation this morning, we both knew what each ingredient was leading up to.

I tapped the table in front of him. *'Whatever happens, I understand. I know you won't believe me, but I've never created a puppet who didn't deserve what was coming.'*

His expression deepened into a scowl, distrust etched in every line of his bronzed face. "You're right. I don't believe you."

I looked at my palm, at the mark of my son, before glancing up at him, swallowing the lump of sorrow in my throat. *'Not all males deserve the same fate.'* I signed, my arms still resting on the table. It had been 12,000 years, but the pain was as raw as the day I lost him.

He swallowed visibly. "I really am sorry about what happened."

I lifted my head entirely, no longer slouched. I wasn't going to linger in that pain—not today. *'I like to play Call of Duty with some males online. We laugh and shout orders at each other. What about you?'*

"I like to play Helldivers and Mortal Kombat." Jackson took the subject change without missing a beat. "Bet I'd wreck you in either." A small, cocky smile played on his lips, and the mood shifted slightly.

'I'm willing to bet I've got more experience than you.' I signed back. I had no idea how old he was, but there were very few immortals older than my sisters and me.

"In real life? Probably." He tilted his head as he looked at me, his dark eyes taking in my features. "It's funny. I watch everyone age to this point and then stop in the pack, but humans keep aging. One day, I'll look in the mirror and realize I'm finally frozen like this."

'How old are you?' I'd not asked before. I'd told him my age but never asked his.

He chuffed and glanced at me. "Thirty-seven. By your standards, I'm probably insignificant."

Gods, he was just barely an immortal! *'At least you're housebroke finally.'*

His slightly lifted expression vanished, his eyes narrowed, and his lips turned down. "Seriously? Why do you have to be such a brat?"

'Because you like it.' I signed with a wink.

He shook his head. "Finish eating so we can get on the road."

Chapter 10

Theia…

Jackson and I drove for a few hours before he finally stopped at a store. "It's cheaper to buy food and cook it, I think. Plus, I have to admit, I'm kinda addicted to your cooking. That is, if you don't mind cooking again."

Was he really asking me? Not ordering or expecting? *'Do you not know how to cook?'* He was young and from a generation that was accustomed to instant gratification. It reminded me of Ella, to be honest. She wouldn't waste time cooking anything as elaborate as the pizza I'd made. She was a spaghetti-from-a-jar kind of person.

"Yeah, but not the shit you cook. Forget it, I'll just buy lunch meat and bread. Fuck." His tone was full of frustration and offense.

102

"Stop," I choked out, earning myself a zap, but I wasn't about to let him spiral, not when he was actually asking me to cook and not being a dick about it.

"What the fuck? You know that shocks you!"

I rolled my eyes. *'Don't get your panties in a twist. I didn't mean to upset you or poke fun. I love to cook and was going to offer to teach you. But if you want to be a dick, then you can sit and drink beer while I enjoy myself.'*

He shifted in his seat, his jaw twitching as he clenched and unclenched. "You haven't really inspired trust with your comments."

A sneaky grin spread across my face. *'Every now and then you gotta throw a dog a bone.'*

He narrowed his eyes, the hint of a smile tugging at his lips. "You know what, you like cooking so much, I might just keep you as my private chef once this is all said and done."

'Eventually, I'd throw a knife at you. You can be a prick.'

"And you can be a brat. Let's get in here, get some food and a cooler. I don't want to keep stopping for food if we don't have to."

'Just say it, mine's better.'

"Old grannies are always the best cooks." His self-assured look pissed me off just a little more than his words, and I flipped him off.

He chuckled. "Nah, you'd like that, wouldn't you, brat?"

Fucking flooded. My panties were soaked at just that one line, and the way the male looked at me, his dark amber eyes, thick hair, high cheekbones, tattoos. *Fuck. Me.* Why was I so hot for my captor? *'You wish.'*

He laughed, unbothered. "Come on, let's go inside instead of sitting out here like a couple of weirdos."

I knew he could smell me, knew he could smell how my body had reacted. Why was I still like this? I should have some sort of curb to my desire after last night, but instead, I was just wanting a damn repeat.

Throwing open the door, I got out, embracing the cooler air. The temperature had dropped in the few days we'd been traveling. How far north had we gone? Granted, it had been unusually warm in Louisiana this year. We'd finally hit December, but it felt like it was in the 50s.

Jackson...

The intoxicating scent of her arousal as we'd gotten out of the Jeep at the store still lingered in my mind. I'd been so

104

consumed with it at the time that I hadn't noticed the rain coming. By the time we'd finished in the store, it was pouring. Now, here I was, in the Jeep with her, that same scent of blood orange and hibiscus hanging in the air, only making the scent of her arousal more mouthwatering. Sweet. Tempting. I had to remind myself that she was a Siren, a weapon. Not someone I should want.

But damn it, something about her pulled at me.

She'd teased me in the store, calling me a dog and not a cat when I told her sushi was about the only thing I didn't like. The memory of how she'd played with that damn lip ring of hers had me shifting in my seat, trying to adjust my throbbing erection. She was an infuriating brat, and I couldn't get enough.

I glanced at the little brat now, only to find her staring at her palm. Guilt twisted my stomach, tempering my desire. I couldn't shake the way it gnawed at me when I remembered how I'd treated her. How I'd put the collar back on her like she was some kind of threat, when she was raw and broken. The way the tears had streamed down her face and the confession she'd made about her child still weighed on me.

She hadn't tried anything. She hadn't tried to escape or fight me. She wasn't what I'd expected from a Siren. There was something more there, buried beneath the surface. The flash of sorrow in her eyes earlier had been enough to twist my heart.

105

I didn't want to admit it, but I could sense her pain. Her past. It was as real as any scar.

"Damn it," I muttered under my breath as the rain turned to sleet, the sound of it pelting the windshield sharp and relentless. I forced myself to focus on the road, pushing everything else out of my mind. The next task. One step closer to breaking the bond.

As we continued to drive, the sleet turned into a full-on ice storm, the wind howling around us, battering the Jeep like a relentless beast. I gripped the wheel tighter as the visibility dropped to nearly nothing. My heart thudded in my chest, every muscle in my body tensed, and instinct screamed at me to get off the road. I'd sensed the shifting weather this morning, but I'd not been predicting this.

"Shit," I muttered, my knuckles turning white as I fought to keep control. The wipers struggled to keep up with the storm, but it was a losing battle. The roads were slick, and the way the sleet lashed against the windshield made it impossible to see more than a few feet ahead.

I glanced at Theia, who was staring out the window with wide eyes that seemed filled with wonder. No trace of fear despite the conditions.

"We're going to stop for the night. We won't make it in these conditions," I said, my voice low. My next move was one I wasn't sure I wanted to do, but I couldn't afford to look away from the road. "Get my phone and turn the GPS to the nearest saved location; that should be the closest safehouse."

She looked at me in shock for a moment before doing what I'd asked. I followed the instructions given, turning off the main road. The wind seemed to scream louder the closer we got, but we made it. What should have been a twenty-minute drive had taken nearly an hour.

As I pulled up to the safehouse, the sleet turned to ice, clinging to the Jeep. "Can you crawl back there and grab the food? I don't want to be running back and forth in this shit to get our stuff." Luckily, we'd put the food in the cooler we'd purchased, so it was easy to carry.

'You are full of requests today. Sure, I'll fetch for you, lazy pup.'

I scowled at her and snapped, "Fuck off with that shit before we get frozen in the Jeep."

She chewed her lip, trying to suppress a giggle that would just end up shocking her. Then she turned and crawled between the seats to grab the cooler. Fuck me, was her ass nice. I turned

107

my head away, looking out the window instead when all I really wanted was to touch her, to grab her thighs and slap her ass.

She turned around and shoved the cooler up at me, followed by the duffle bag that held both our clothes. Then she crawled back into the front. *'Go get the door like a good boy, I don't have the keys.'*

With a small snarl of frustration, I grabbed the duffle and opened my door. "Get the cooler, and let's go." Goddess, I wanted to put her in her place. If she were really my mate, I'd have fucked her right there in the Jeep, ice storm be damned. But she wasn't. The bond I felt with her was her spell, her Siren's call that was dark and twisted and enslaved males.

We made it inside, and she went straight to the kitchen with the cooler and began putting things in the fridge. She straightened and smiled.

'I'm going to change into dry clothes, then cook, and you are helping me.' She signed as she crossed the room and grabbed the duffle bag.

It didn't take long for her to come back out in dry clothing and make a beeline for the kitchen. She began rummaging through the cabinets before she pulled out a 9x13 baking dish. *'Set the oven to 375. We are cooking the salmon until it is flaky.*

Coat the salmon, spinach, cherry tomatoes, and cream cheese in salt, pepper, olive oil, and a little lemon juice.'

I watched as she put everything in the pan, pulling the cherry tomatoes off the stems. She'd sectioned the salmon on one side, the tomatoes in the middle, and the spinach on the other end. After that, she pulled out a pot and started boiling water for the noodles she'd bought. *'We'll check the salmon once the noodles are done, it should be about right.'*

I watched as she rubbed oil around the rim of the pot before it began boiling and frowned. "Why did you do that? It's not like the pot is going to stick to anything."

'It helps to keep it from boiling over. Oil and water don't mix.'

I was surprised to see that she was right and the water didn't boil over like noodles usually did. She never put a spoon on top or anything. The meal was quick and delicious. Through the whole process she would sign teasing remarks, her bratty personality always present.

Theia...

After we finished eating, I was ready for a shower to relax some of the tension in my body. While Jackson hadn't been too much of a prick, I found myself almost enjoying his company *and*

109

more than enjoying watching him. He was a predator, and I loved it. The way he held himself and the constant hungry look in his eyes kept my body aching for him. I needed a shower.

'Be a good dog and do the dishes, don't just lick them clean either. I'm taking a shower," I signed, unable to resist the urge to poke fun at him.

"I'd tell you to wash the brat off like last night, but I don't think that's possible," he shot back as he got to his feet and collected the dishes.

I leaned back in my chair, watching Jackson as he carried the dishes to the sink. His movements were fluid, powerful, and predatory. I should have been disgusted by the way he carried himself, by the way his muscles flexed beneath his shirt, but I wasn't.

I was fascinated.

Damn him.

He caught me staring, a slow, knowing smirk curving on his lips. "Something on your mind, brat?"

I schooled my features, lifting my hands lazily. *'Just admiring how well-trained you are. Good boy.'*

His smirk sharpened. He dried his hands on a towel before turning and stepping toward me with unhurried confidence. The space between us evaporated, my breath catching as he planted a hand on the table beside me, leaning down so close I could feel the heat radiating off him.

"Careful," he murmured, his voice thick with amusement and something darker. "Keep teasing me, and you might end up on your knees, showing me just how good you can be."

Heat flooded my core, but I refused to let him see it. Instead, I let my lips curve into a slow, taunting smile. *'That would require me wanting you that much.'*

His eyes flashed with challenge, but instead of pushing, he stepped back. "Go take your shower, Theia. Before you start trembling."

I clenched my jaw, refusing to acknowledge the way my skin burned as I pushed up from the chair. I wouldn't look at him again, knowing damn well he could smell my desire.

By the time I reached the bathroom, I was cursing myself. I turned on the water, bracing my hands against the sink. My reflection stared back at me, lips parted, pupils dilated.

This was dangerous. I shouldn't want him.

But Gods help me, I did.

The thought of his body, how he'd touched me last night—*all of it*—swirled in my head. My mind had gone there so many times today that I'd practically been torturing myself.

Not that I expected a repeat. He hated me for what I was. I shouldn't be attracted to him, either. He was holding me captive. I stepped into the shower and pulled the curtain shut, the scraping of the metal hooks over the rod echoing in my mind as I remembered how he'd ordered me to look at him while I came.

Nope. Stop it. I scolded myself as I lathered up my hair. I focused on working the conditioner into my hair instead of the large, sexy male in the other room. Then I began soaping up my body, my hands sliding over my skin, and fuck me if it didn't make me think of how his fingers had slipped so easily inside me.

I was standing under the hot spray, rinsing the soap off, trying to forget what it had felt like to have his fingers inside me and his weight on top of me, but it wasn't fucking working. The itch in my throat was still raging. I'd orgasmed, how was it still present?

The sound of the door opening made me peek my head out of the shower. Jackson was pulling his shirt over his head as he kicked the door shut behind him. My eyes widened, and I pulled the curtain shut. Was I hallucinating? No, I heard his pants hit the floor, and I held my breath.

"Are you finished washing yet, brat?" he asked from the other side of the curtain. What was he waiting on? Did I want him in here with me?

112

"Or do you need me to do it for you?" He pulled the curtain back and climbed in. "Because all I've been able to think about is what your fucking body would feel like covered in soap, my hands slipping over every curve, my fingers tracing every tattoo. I've had to smell you all fucking day long, and now I want to touch you."

'Touch only,' I signed, hating how much I wanted the male who was holding me captive. The male who was probably plotting my death once the bond was severed.

"Such a bossy little thing, aren't you?" He stepped up to me, his eyes taking in my every movement, like he was waiting for something. "Let's see if you can follow orders enough to get your own little reward." His lips quirked into a grin that promised wicked things just as he stepped up to me and sank to his knees.

"Spread your legs like a good little brat and let me taste you."

'If I say no, then what?' The question flowed from my hands in sign language. I reveled in the sight of him before me, brought to his knees, his body stripped down bare. Every tattoo and muscle was on display for my eyes, while his erection, hard and prominent, bobbed between his legs.

"Then I kick you out of the shower and finish myself off while you get nothing." His hands slid up my thighs and cupped

113

the cheeks of my ass. "But we both know that's not how this is going to play out, so be a good little brat and let me have my dessert."

He was giving me a choice, just like when he'd held back last night, waiting for me to agree. Yes, he'd pushed, but he was a Lycan, a male driven by scent and instinct. In all reality, I probably was his mate, and from what I'd heard, Lycans were known to be unable to resist their mates. Did I want to allow this? Every fiber of my being screamed to touch him. This sexy, dark male kneeling before me, my captor.

Despite the paradox, I instinctively shifted, creating the necessary space for him.

"Good girl," he growled just before his mouth was on me. My head fell back as his tongue plunged inside me. It wasn't long before I felt the jerking of his shoulder, and I glanced down to see his fist pumping his cock while his face was buried between my legs. My breathing became heavy, my fingers locked in his hair, and my body coiled with delicious tension.

I came apart on his tongue, his one hand gripping my ass in a nearly painful hold, his other pumping him to his own release. "Yes, cum for me, Theia," he said against my flesh. He wasn't far behind me. I could feel the tension in his body as he

114

buried his face in my thigh, kissing and nipping as a guttural sound left his lips.

He gave a soft laugh. "You never answered me. Have you finished washing yet?"

He pushed to his feet, shoving his dark, wet hair out of his face, and I couldn't resist what I did next. I stepped forward, placing my hands on his chest, and licked the water running down his neck as I rose onto my toes. His hands gripped my elbows, and he groaned, pulling me slightly closer to him.

He pushed my back against the shower wall again, looking down at me as water ran off his dark face onto mine. "Careful doing things like that."

I stood there, chest heaving, my body betraying me. I knew what I was doing. I knew what this kiss would mean. But my mind was clouded with the need to touch him, to feel him, to erase the gap between us. Without thinking, I pulled him down to me, tasting his lips like they were my only lifeline. I was fucking *starved* for him. I didn't care that I was his captive. Didn't care that he was thinking of how to kill me. I just needed *him*. I needed to feel whatever it was he made me feel.

His tongue slipped into my mouth, deepening the kiss. Our hands roamed each other's bodies, searching for the perfect place to cling to as we pressed our naked, wet forms together. My breath came in ragged gasps, my focus narrowing to the way his body melded against mine—the raw, undeniable need burning in his eyes. His heat seared into me, his lean frame taut against mine, but it wasn't enough. I needed *more*.

Suddenly, he broke the kiss, bracing an arm against the shower wall beside my head. "Fuck, Theia, we can't do that, or I'll lose control. You have no idea what you did when you entrapped me. My wolf thinks you're mine, even if I know the truth. And all I want is to wreck you in every way imaginable."

I pulled away from him with trembling hands, the taste of him still lingering on my lips. I stood there for a heartbeat longer, my chest rising and falling in a desperate attempt to steady myself. The water streamed between us, the only sound in the room, yet it felt like the world was closing in.

The sting of his rejection snapped me back to reality. I needed to get out of the shower, to put distance between us—fast. *'Thanks for the release,'* I signed.

With that, I slipped away from him and out of the shower, leaving him under the spray.I didn't bother telling him he wasn't entrapped; that I was more than likely his true mate and he was rejecting me. To him, I was nothing more than his prisoner. His words had hit me like a blow, and I wasn't sure what unsettled me more—the promise in his voice or the terror that came with it. He

116

wanted to take me. I knew it. But did I want that too, knowing what it meant? My heart pounded in my chest, not from fear but from the dangerous pull I felt toward him.

I grabbed a towel and wrapped it around myself, refusing to look back. But I felt him and his gaze searing into my skin, the energy between us thrumming like a live wire, dangerous and unrelenting.

I needed space. Distance. Anything to remind myself that he was my captor.

But as I stepped out of the bathroom, the heat of his mouth still lingering on my skin, I knew it wouldn't be enough.

Not nearly enough.

Chapter 11

Jackson...

I barely stopped myself from punching the wall as Theia stepped out of the shower.

What the fuck had I even said to her? *I'd wreck her*? What was wrong with me? Why had I admitted anything? And what the hell was I supposed to think of her response: *thanks for the release*?

Goddess, I was so fucking stupid.

She was out there now, not chained to the futon. No restraints.

Would she run? Maybe. But the ice storm we'd just driven through would stop her. She wouldn't get far. The thought helped calm my fears, just a little.

I washed quickly, my movements rough with frustration, and stepped out. A towel was wrapped around my hips as I hadn't taken clothes into the bathroom with me. Hell, I'd followed her in without thinking twice.

One whiff of her arousal, and I'd lost all control. Her scent filled the air, thick and intoxicating. It was everywhere, and it was *everything*. She'd been teasing me all damn day, until finally the smell of her had driven me to the edge. I hadn't been able to resist it.

When I entered the living room, I found her logging into the gaming console.

"What the fuck do you think you're doing?" I demanded, storming over to her and yanking the controller from her hands. I'd just given her a chance—*a chance*—to call for help, for other Sirens to come and save her. To entrap me.

'You said you liked Mortal Kombat, I thought we could play. I'm bored,' she signed with an irritated look on her face. *'Guess that's too intimate for the same jackass who just had his face between my legs.'*

My gaze flicked to the screen, and sure enough, Mortal Kombat was pulled up. She wasn't calling for help. It was just a game.

"I'm always player one. Get the other controller while I get dressed, brat."

119

'Bull shit. You thought I was calling for help. Guess what, mutt, I have no one to contact. Everyone I game with is mortal.'

"Good, that means I don't have to kill anyone today," I tossed back, refusing to let the guilt eat at me; not when her seaglass eyes were looking at me with that accusation. I wouldn't admit she was right.

I turned and went to the bedroom, holding the damp towel around my hips. She was watching me with such intensity that I could feel her eyes on my skin. Even with the door shut, I could still feel her gaze like she could see through the damn wood. Dropping my towel, I pulled on a pair of jogging pants before heading back out.

I had to get my head straight. Maybe playing a game would help. I needed the distraction from the urge to pick up where that kiss had left off. Every instinct in my body screamed at me to take her, to mark her as mine. I knew better. It wasn't real. It couldn't be. It was just her Siren magic sinking its claws into me, twisting me up in ways I had no control over.

When I stalked back into the living room, I found her right where I left her—fuming on the couch.

"You ready to have your ass handed to you?" I wasn't sure if I was trying to lighten the mood or push her further, but the words were out before I reached the sofa.

'Let's see if your skills are as pathetic as your trash talk, mutt,' she shot back. Her face was still etched with frustration, her hands moving with sharp, clipped motions.

As I walked to the couch and settled in, I could see the challenge in her eyes. Her constant rebellion was something I couldn't decide if I loved or hated. She refused to back down, and refused to be cowed. It had been five days, and she still didn't act like a captive. Instead, she was cocky and snarky.

"Let's see if your skills can back up that attitude of yours," I said, grabbing the second controller and wiggling it at her, my lips curling into a dark grin.

She shot me a sideways glance as she took the controller with a small yank. *'Try not to cry when I crush you.'*

I arched a brow. "Keep talking, brat. You'll need more than sass to beat me."

Theia...

As Jackson and I gamed, the tension between us seemed to dissipate. It was replaced with playful elbowing, each of us trying to knock the controller out of the other's hand. By the time

121

we called it a night, I'd lost track of who had won the most times. I'd actually had fun with the Lycan during the hours we'd played.

When he called lights out, I'd been ready for him to chain me to the futon again. Instead, he directed me to the bedroom, where I discovered bunk beds. It felt strange to sleep in a bed without my wrist cuffed for the first time in days. I couldn't help but wonder if this meant he was changing his mind about killing me or if he was just confident I had nowhere to go.

Morning came too quickly. I woke up to the faint sound of movement outside the bedroom and the smell of coffee wafting through the open door. For a moment, I lay there, disoriented, the quiet of the morning feeling strange after the chaos of the last few days. I hadn't expected to fall asleep so quickly or so deeply, but the exhaustion from everything had caught up with me.

Rubbing my eyes, I hesitated to climb out of bed. It was warm and comfortable, even if it wasn't mine. The pull of that cup of heaven, though, was too strong to ignore any longer. I tossed back the blankets and climbed out of bed.

My eyes drifted to my palm, where the seahorse, Theo's soul, had been every morning of my existence. *Mommy loves you,* I thought quietly before leaving the room and making my way to the kitchen.

"Morning, brat. Once we eat and get dressed, we need to hit the road. We've still got a couple of hours before we reach the address the Priestess sent me."

'Where are we going?' I signed, then moved to the coffee pot.

"To get Gorgon scales and Centaur hooves. Apparently, the Gorgon we're looking for is a dealer on the black market." I could see the twitch in his jaw and the tension lining his body as he spoke.

'Can it really be called a black market when immortals don't have the same laws as humans or anyone to enforce them?' I signed, watching him carefully. I wanted to see if his reaction was to the black market itself, or to the Gorgon we were going to see—an immortal female who held power over males, just like me.

"The Immortal black market has its place—dealing in hard-to-come-by items. Think about it: how many Centaurs do you think are willing to cut off their hooves for a spell?"

'It will grow back, but I understand; the pain is terrible. Immortals are usually immune to infection, but not pain.' So it was the methods he disagreed with.

"Exactly. Then again, *you* did rip your own throat out," he said, shooting me a sideways glance.

123

I didn't have a comeback for that, so I just stared at him as I drank my coffee. The truth was, in that moment, I'd been so raw with pain from my memories and dreams that I'd wanted to escape everything. There were more days than I cared to admit when I wanted nothing more than to stop existing. Yes, time had blurred some memories for my sisters and me—but not that one. I would never forget the loss of my son. The day Atlantis fell was seared into my soul, a wound that would never fade.

"**A**nyway," he sighed, the weight of the morning still hanging between us, "do you want to make breakfast, or should I?"

'I'll make it,' I signed, grateful for the change in subject.

We'd fallen into silence after that. Jackson packed up our things while I made bacon and eggs with the groceries he'd picked up yesterday. When we left the safehouse, I was relieved to see that the ice had started to melt. The temperature was rising, just enough to chase away the snow and slick roads.

Jackson didn't speak to me until we were about to pull onto the main road. "When we get there, you need to be careful. I have no idea what we're walking into, but I'm pretty sure it's not the kind of place where you should test boundaries. We need to at least *appear* to have each other's backs."

'I'm not an idiot. This is the black market, and I've already got the whole "pet" vibe going, thanks to this collar.' The bitterness was etched on my face, even if he couldn't hear it in my sign language.

"Glad to see you understand," he said, pulling away from the stop sign and onto the main road.

We drove like that for a few hours, with only the radio breaking the silence. Jackson seemed done talking to me after yesterday. Not that we needed to bond or anything—after all, I was his captive, and he saw me as a plague to all males. Still, being left alone with my thoughts wasn't exactly fun.

I was drowning in guilt over Kassie, over my desire to end it all when this was done. What choice did I have, though? Jackson had told me that I should be dead, that his pack had made it their mission to eradicate my kind. I'd lived for so long and with so much pain that the thought of death beckoned me like a good night's sleep after a long day, especially when I looked at my palm.

"We're here. Keep your head down and stay close to me. If you make me, I'll put the cuffs on, but I'd rather not do that in a place like this." Jackson pulled into a dead-end alley that didn't quite look right, then drove through a solid wall, heading down into an underground parking garage.

125

The parking garage opened into an underground cavern, dimly lit by magical floating orbs that cast an eerie glow. As we opened the doors to get out, I was hit with the earthy scent of the cavern, mixed with the sharp tang of oil and the faint, unpleasant hint of rot and decay. Across the 'garage,' a lone door stood, with a Wraith flickering in and out of sight, its form barely visible in the dim light.

"Stay close to me, and don't make eye contact with anyone. We don't want to draw unnecessary attention to you, especially without your power." Jackson's hand settled on my lower back as he gently guided me toward the door.

Now wasn't the time to test my luck, not with a Wraith watching. I swallowed my pride and allowed him to guide me. While my sisters and I were stronger than most Sirens and adept in various fighting skills, there was nothing we could do against a Wraith. Most immortals were powerless against the shadowy creatures. They had no form, no heartbeat—only a cold, misty presence that they could solidify at will.

The Wraith flickered out of the way as we passed through the door, but the chill of its presence still brushed against my neck and cheek, as though it had reached out and touched me. I suppressed the shiver and walked fully into what was a hidden bazaar. The massive underground warehouse was filled with

126

winding pathways, hidden alcoves, and stacked crates of illicit goods.

'Do you know where we're going in here?' I signed, taking in the vastness of the place.

There were booths with shady merchants of all varieties, some having humanoid appearances, while others were grotesque and clearly unable to blend in with mortals. To my disgust, there was even a Grunch sleeping in a cage behind one of the stalls, as though it were being sold as some sort of bloodthirsty pet.

"I'd say it's the door with the Gorgon leaning against it," Jackson's dry response drew my attention away from the creature in the cage. His hand remained on my lower back, guiding me through the maze of stalls and immortals. Jars of questionable contents and books that appeared to be bound in different types of flesh were on display among the tabletops as we passed by.

"Well, well, what do we have here? A puppy... and his chew toy," the Gorgon cooed with a tilt of her full lips. Her deadly eyes were hidden behind designer sunglasses, preventing Jackson and other males from being turned to stone. Deep copper and burnt gold snakes adorned her head, and though her eyes were concealed, there was no doubt her hair would have been red or auburn. Her grey business suit was tailored to perfection, the jacket left open, with a white shirt beneath.

127

"I was told to speak with Deedra," Jackson said, his voice tight. I could feel the tension in his body as he stood beside me.

Her head tilted, and the copper and gold serpents flicked their black tongues, tasting the air. I couldn't help but wonder if she could see through their eyes as well. "Let's step inside my office and discuss business, then, shall we?" She moved with fluid grace through the door, not bothering to check if we followed, but her snakes kept their gaze fixed on us, on everything.

The room was dressed like an office, but it felt more like a butcher's prep station—clinical, cold, and waiting for its next victim. Behind the desk was a safe large enough to fit not one, but two bodies, and a smaller lockbox sat in the corner.

"Would either of you like a drink? I have some of the finest scotch." The confidence and authority seeping from her reminded me of Cleopatra.

"I'm here for Gorgon scales and Centaur hooves," Jackson announced, his tone even, betraying nothing, though I could still feel the tension in his body.

Deedra cocked her head to the side, her snakes flicking with interest. "Straight to business, then? How... boring." She settled into the chair behind the desk, lacing her fingers under her chin. "What makes you think I'm offering these items?"

128

Jackson arched an eyebrow, crossing his arms over his chest as he finally removed his hand from my back. "You're a Gorgon. You have at least one of the items I need, and I was told you'd have the Centaur hooves as well."

A seductive smile spread across the Gorgon's lips. "You have contacts, but no sources. How delightfully entertaining. I *suppose* I could assist with the procurement of these items. My price is steep, though. Are you prepared to pay it?"

"Name it."

"You want a piece of me, and I want a piece of you, Lycan," she purrs, her voice dripping with mockery and challenge. Her lips curl into a slow, predatory smile. "Turn those hands for me, let me see your paws. I just need one."

Jackson stiffened, his jaw tightening as a low growl rumbled in his throat. I instinctively stepped closer to him, my fingers brushing his arm in a subtle gesture of restraint.

Deedra chuckled, a soft, throaty sound, as she reclined back, crossing one leg over the other. "Oh, don't tell me you're shy. Big, bad wolf, afraid of a little snip? It's not permanent, and I'll even let you keep it when it grows back. Consider it... a token of our little exchange."

Jackson shifted his weight, tension rolling off him in waves. His voice was cold and measured, but beneath it simmered barely contained fury. "You're asking me to cut off my own hand."

Deedra's smile didn't falter, but her eyes sharpened behind her designer shades. She tilted her head, resting her chin delicately on her palm. "Hand? Is that what you call it? I call it leverage, my dear. A symbol of trust. Besides…" Her voice dropped, soft and intimate, as she leaned in. "A Lycan's paw is so rare. So… *personal*."

I signed quickly to Jackson, my fingers moving with edge. *'We could always rip her head off and take the scales that way.'* I didn't like this and I didn't trust her.

Deedra's expression cooled. Her eyes flicked to me, her tone laced with venom. "Careful, Siren. This is between me and your pet."

She stood, gliding toward Jackson. Her heels clicked softly on the stone floor, a quiet, deliberate threat. "So, what will it be, Lycan? Shall we seal our deal… or shall I find someone else to amuse me?"

"How do I know you have everything I'm looking for? You never even confirmed your name." Jackson asked as though he were honestly considering cutting off his own hand.

Deedra pulled open a drawer and withdrew a pair of garden shears—worn, but wickedly sharp. The blackened metal

130

caught the dim light, the edges gleaming with lethal promise. She weighed them in her hand, gave a soft hum of approval, and smiled like a predator about to feed.

"You'd be surprised how often I need to do this," she mused, as if she were merely pruning a hedge instead of preparing to mutilate a part of herself.

One of the copper-scaled serpents curled in protest as she grasped it. The creature hissed and thrashed, its forked tongue flicking wildly, but Deedra held firm. With a sigh of irritation, she positioned the shears at the base of its writhing body, right where it merged with her scalp.

"Stay still, darling," she crooned, almost affectionately just before snapping the shears shut.

A sharp snap split the air, followed by a wet, muted squelch as steel met sinew. A few droplets of dark ichor splattered across the desk, one trailing slowly down Deedra's temple. The severed snake landed with a soft, twitching thud, still curling in slow, mindless coils.

Deedra didn't flinch. Instead, she reached up with practiced ease, smearing a thumb through the slick line of blood. With a slow, deliberate smirk, she licked it clean, like it was nothing more than spilled wine.

"There. Straight from the source." She gave a cruel little smile, spinning the copper-scaled segment between her fingers before flicking it toward Jackson. "Don't misplace it. Regrowth isn't exactly speedy."

I glanced at Jackson to see his jaw twitch and his nostrils flare. Neither of us had been expecting that. Granted, I was used to Ella's regular self-mutilation. Could Jackson do it? Could I watch him do it? I'd not been able to watch Ella or even enter her bathroom during her hours of vulnerability, lying in the tub, soaked in her own blood, her neck sliced open like a gaping maw.

Deedra pulled out a butcher knife and set it on the table. "Shall I do the honors? Or would your, silent little friend here like to do it?"

'Show us the hooves,' I signed quickly, not wanting any part of this exchange.

She clicked her tongue. "Not until his mitts shift, *pet*."

Jackson pulled his belt from his waist, the sharp snap of leather cutting through the air, louder than I'd have expected, considering the low hum of activity just beyond the heavy metal door. He stepped up to me, his eyes flicking to Deedra before settling back on mine. "Listen up, brat. I need you to get this tight, or I'll pass out from blood loss. Got it?"

I narrowed my eyes at him. *'I've done this before, believe it or not.'*

"How interesting, the delicate little Siren is more hardened than she appears." Deedra pulled a key from her pocket and unlocked the lock box. "Does that mean you will be liberating my prize from the handsome hound?"

I shook my head without looking at her, focusing on pulling the belt as tight as I could around Jackson's lower arm.

"I'd have thought you would be simply swooning for the opportunity, seeing as you've got that lovely collar on. Or are these items to assist in its removal?"

"Information wasn't part of the deal. Now chop-chop, Gorgon."

Jackson cut off her teasing, one hand gripping the arm of the chair while the other—clawed and fur-covered—rested on the desk, an offering to the twisted bitch across from him.

Without warning, Deedra hefted the knife and brought the blade down.

Metal struck metal with a piercing clang, the sound ringing in my skull like a struck bell.

Then came the part I'd never forget—the sickening snap of bone, followed by the wet, sucking tear of flesh and tendon as the blade severed his wrist. Blood gushed from the stump, a hot

133

spray that splattered across the edge of the desk. Deedra slid the severed paw aside like a used napkin in a casual, almost bored manner.

Jackson's body seized. A vicious snarl ripped from his throat, deep and raw, more beast than man. His claws gouged into the chair's armrest, the metal groaning and protesting before snapping like cheap plastic under the immense power of his grip.

His breath tore from him in harsh, uneven bursts, his nostrils flaring, teeth bared and dripping. For a moment, I thought he might lunge at her as he shot to his feet. His eyes flashed gold, his whole body vibrating with fury, but when his wounded arm twitched, agony sent him staggering back instead.

I caught him just before he dropped, my hands slipping in his blood as I fought to keep him upright.

"Get—get the items."

His weight bore down on me, the smell of blood thick in the air, sharp and metallic as it mingled with his woodsy scent.

"Best to get yourself under control before going back out there. Looks like this is your first time experiencing this kind of pain." Deedra placed a sack on the table and dropped the snake inside, followed by a hoof from the lock box she'd just opened. Next, she deposited a box of medical supplies on the desk, blocking the flow of blood from reaching the canvas sack. "I'd

134

say you have a few minutes before losing consciousness. Go ahead and wrap it so no one slips in the blood."

I shot a glare at her and urged Jackson back into the seat, intending to wrap it as she'd said. "Grab-the-shit," he grated out at me.

"She can't when she has her arms full of you. Try to regulate your breathing, you'll hold onto consciousness longer while she gathers your things and wraps that for you. There are creatures out there that would love to collect more than a paw."

Was she actually being nice? Like Ella, when she corrected our form after kicking our ass in a fight. The momentary shock wore off as a low growl slipped from Jackson, and I felt him release me as he sank into the chair once more. With skilled movements honed over centuries of wound care, I bandaged him, the blood quickly dampening the bandages, and then grabbed the bag.

Deedra's hand slipped beneath the desk, and a buzzing sound filled my ears for a moment before the bookcase on the back wall slid open.

"That tunnel takes you around the corner to the warehouse entrance, on the inside. It won't get you out, but it'll improve your chances. Ta-ta now." She wiggled her fingers at us, already

135

moving toward the door, her boots clicking against the floor in a casual, unbothered rhythm.

"I hate her," Jackson huffed, pushing himself to his feet and staggering toward the bookcase. I was at his side in an instant, steadying him.

"Fuck off, I'm fine," he growled, his voice harsh and strained as he tried to push me away.

I reached out and pinched him, shooting him a sharp glare. Blood was already dripping from his bandaged arm.

"Ow! Fuck, what the hell?"

"We need to leave fast. Let me help get us out of here."

He staggered into the wall as the bookcase slid shut behind us, breathing hard. I caught him before he could slump further.

"Fine."

Wrapping my arms around Jackson, I helped shoulder his weight as we pushed through the narrow, dimly lit tunnel. The faint hum of the single overhead light every few feet was the only sound, aside from the occasional drip of Jackson's blood and his labored, shallow breaths. The tunnel felt like it was closing in, the walls pressing in on us with every step, and I could feel Jackson's weight dragging on me more and more.

As we neared the end of the passage, the faint hum of the bazaar outside grew louder. The last section of the tunnel plunged us into near darkness, the lights stopping and giving way to blackness for a few feet before a sliver of light pierced the void. I glanced up at him, worry twisting in my gut as I noticed the shallow rise and fall of his chest.

"Keep moving." His voice was weak; I could tell he was struggling to hold onto consciousness.

We stepped out into the light and noise of the market, and I immediately scanned the area. No one appeared to be following us, but the weight of our proximity to danger was still heavy. We weren't safe yet.

The Wraith came out of nowhere. Its form flickered in the shadows, and I felt its cold presence before I even saw it. Drawn to Jackson's vulnerability, the creature swarmed toward us, its lifeless eyes glowing with hunger.

"Back off!" I choked out, my voice muffled by the zap of the collar. I shoved us through the Wraith's shifting form, dragging Jackson as if we were wading through thick mud. The Wraith hesitated, its attention distracted by Jackson's bloodied state, but it relented just long enough for us to reach the Jeep.

I opened the passenger door and helped him in, guiding his limp body into the seat.

Jackson reached forward for the steering wheel, his eyes unfocused, confusion clouding his face. "What—what's going on? I need to get us out of here."

I shook my head, pointing to my chest and shaking his keys at him, which I had grabbed from his pocket as I helped him sit. His eyes flickered to them for a moment before he lurched forward, reaching for them. I pushed him back, surprised by the force he managed to muster despite his condition.

"Give me my keys," he snarled, his voice raw.

"I—drive," I choked out through the collar, the words mangled and strained. I shook my head again, panic rising in my chest as I tried to make him understand.

"Fuck. Even blurry, you're beautiful," he muttered, shaking his head. "Don't wreck my Jeep."

He leaned his head back against the seat, his eyes fluttering closed. I had to shove his leg and arm inside the Jeep before I could close the door. By the time I reached the other side, he was unconscious, blood soaking through the bandages on his arm and dripping into his lap.

I bit my lip, glancing nervously at the Wraith still lingering by the entrance. Its form flickered toward us, drawn to Jackson's blood and his weakened state. If it came any closer, it would drain him completely. I couldn't let that happen. What if it

138

turned on me next? I had no way to defend myself against one of them.

My heart hammered in my chest as I tried to steady my breathing. I needed to act fast. With a hard swallow, I reached into his back pocket for his phone. He shifted just enough for me to pull it free, wiping the blood off his thumb, praying it would unlock the screen.

It did.

I quickly went to the GPS, my fingers trembling as I scrolled through his saved locations and selected the nearest one. I hit "Start" and felt a flicker of hope when the directions appeared. With a glance back at Jackson, I started the engine and set the Jeep into motion, praying I'd find the safehouse before the Wraith could pick up Jackson's scent and act on its desires—or come after me.

<u>Chapter 12</u>

Theia...

I pulled into the driveway that the GPS had led me to. Glancing over at Jackson, I steeled myself for what I was about to do. This was my chance to escape. I hadn't been able to leave him while the Wraith was there. They were the only creatures that truly terrified me, not for my own sake, but for the soul of my son, still tucked into the center of my palm.

Getting out of the Jeep, I circled to the passenger side and gently opened the door. All I had to do was unlock the collar the way I had unlocked his phone; then I could leave him propped against the safehouse.

Reaching in, I lifted his remaining hand and fumbled to get his thumb up before putting it to my throat. There was an audible click as the collar released.

And then his fingers shifted.

140

They slid over my skin, curling around my neck with practiced ease, without him even opening his eyes.

"If you wanted a necklace," he murmured, "you could've just asked."

My breath caught as my heart sped up. I'd assumed he was out cold.

His eyes opened slowly, glowing with something far too lucid.

"Why are you wanting the collar off, brat?" he asked, and his grip tightened just enough to remind me that even bleeding, even broken, he was still in control.

My mouth was dry, but I forced the words out. "We're at the safehouse. I need the code to get us in."

His thumb brushed against my pulse, and I hated that it jumped at his touch.

"Mm." He looked past me at the building, then back at my face. "Put the collar back on. I lost a hand, not my brain."

His grip loosened on my throat as if to allow me to snap the collar back on, which now rested on the back of my neck.

I didn't move.

Maybe I could run. Perhaps he wouldn't catch me.

141

"Don't," he said before I even made a decision. "Try it, and I'll chase you. I will catch you, and I won't be nearly as nice the second time."

I swallowed and rolled my eyes. "Can you even walk?"

"Put the fucking collar on," he growled. "I lost my hand, not my foot."

"Maybe I like your hand better," I said against his tightening grip. A stupid part of me really did like the way his warm, callused fingers felt pressing in around my throat—just enough pressure to make speech hard but allow me to breathe.

"I could just rip your vocal cords out and pack your limp ass inside," he replied.

A huff left my lips before I reached up and clicked the collar back into place, his hand sliding out of the way. When his hand dropped away, I stood up and told myself I didn't miss it. Glancing at the cooler in the back seat, I signed, *'I'll grab the cooler first, then come back out for our bags. You're no good with one hand.'*

"Such a bossy little brat," he muttered as he got out of the Jeep and staggered a step before righting himself and heading toward the door of the safehouse.

The blood loss must have left him light-headed, even if he had somehow held onto consciousness. If I ran now, I had no idea

142

how to remove the collar. The number of people who knew ASL was limited. I grabbed the cooler out of the back and followed him to the safehouse as I thought through my options.

"I can see you thinking. If you run, I'll come after you. My wolf won't let you go until this magical bond you created is severed." His voice yanked me out of my thoughts. He was leaning against the side of the safehouse, watching me as I packed the cooler.

"I'm not going to run. I'll help you sever the bond," I signed, sliding the cooler up on my arm to free both hands. Telling him I hadn't entrapped him was pointless. He wouldn't believe me, and I wasn't sure I wanted him to find out I was really his mate. If we could get the bond severed, then good. I didn't need that complication in my life.

Jackson...

I'd watched as Theia brought everything into the house before locking the door. She'd said she wouldn't run, but I still didn't trust her. She'd needed me to get out of the black market, but now she didn't need me.

What the hell had I been thinking when I'd been intimate with her? I'd given her exactly what she wanted. I'd fed a fucking

143

Siren. I was disgusted with myself, yet I still found myself wanting to do it again and again.

'You said you heal when you shift, so shift. Stop suffering,' she signed as she stood in the kitchen. *'I'll cook something to eat while you do your dog thing. It's lunchtime.'*

I narrowed my eyes and watched as she moved, unpacking the cooler. Could I change? In my wolf form, I was less vulnerable, but this would be the first time I'd changed to heal like this. I'd had broken bones and wounds, but never a severed limb.

She turned to face me and rolled her eyes before signing, *'What are you waiting for? It's not like I can escape with this on my neck. Just shift so you can maybe be a little less shitty.'*

Without any further hesitation, I began stripping. Pulling my bad arm through my sleeve proved to be excruciating, but I managed to do it, then proceeded to pull it over my head. After kicking off my shoes, I unbuttoned my pants, which was a lot harder with one hand, and stepped out of them.

Through the entire thing, I watched her, loving how her eyes widened as she took me in. The little angry look that had been painted on her face was replaced with one of silent hunger. Her seaglass eyes lingered on my tattoos before dragging down my body in silent appraisal. *Fuck, I want her.*

"Put my clothes in the washer like a good brat," I said before shifting. The magic transformation prickled over my body, like pins and needles, followed by warmth and popping as my body transformed from humanoid to wolf. My body tingled as hair covered every inch of me and everything felt tight, like I needed a good stretch. Three paws hit the floor, while the last one remained missing, though the pain had significantly decreased.

'If you shit on the floor, I'm rubbing your nose in it—even if you are a three-legged dog,' she signed after I finished shifting. I bared my teeth at her before staggering a step in her direction. *'Bad dog, sit. You're still hurt.'*

Goddess help me! The female was infuriating, stubborn, and rebellious, and I fucking *loved* it.

Sitting down with a huff, I glared at her like a predator watching its prey. She rolled her eyes and pulled her shirt over her head, throwing it in the pile with my clothes before moving to the sink and washing up to her elbows. I watched, curious as to why she'd stripped and more than a little transfixed by her nearly naked body.

My eyes tracked every line of ink etched into her skin—tattoos sprawling across her chest, curling over her shoulders, winding down her arms and back. I followed the trail of roses that climbed her spine and bloomed across her shoulder

145

blades as she moved around the kitchen. The artist had left out the thorns—an oversight, in my opinion. They would have suited her.

The closer I looked at the tattoos, the more I saw what they were hiding. Beneath the twisting vines and blooms were scars—deep ones—on her arms, crossing like whip lines across her back.

The fur along my spine rose. A growl rumbled low in my chest, unbidden, as the image of what must have happened to her took shape. She had been abused *before* her immortality, when she was still vulnerable. Still mortal.

She turned then, brow cocked and lips curled into that familiar bite of attitude.

'*What the hell is your problem? I'm cooking you dinner, dickhead,*' she signed one-handed, the spatula still in her other hand.

I stared at my missing paw. It wasn't like I could respond—wasn't like I had any right to. I couldn't ask her where those scars came from. I couldn't fix them, and I shouldn't want to.

I slid forward and laid down between her and the door. Maybe it was the blood loss, maybe the pain, but my head was spinning. I closed my eyes and listened to the soft, steady sounds

146

of her moving around the kitchen, like she wasn't a threat. Like this was normal.

I woke to the clink of a plate being placed in front of me. Blinking open my eyes, I lifted my head, the rich and savory smell of food filling my nostrils. She'd placed a plate of grilled chicken, quinoa, and stir-fried vegetables in front of me.

She sat cross-legged on the floor a few feet away, still in just her pants and a bra, completely unbothered by my presence, the collar still snug around her throat.

She lifted her hands and signed, calm and casual. *'Eat. You lost a lot of blood. This will help you heal. I'm taking a shower after this and washing our clothes, but only if you beg like a good dog.'*

My ears flicked. My tail didn't move. But if I had the strength, I might have growled—or maybe laughed. Her mouth curved faintly as she picked up her own plate and started to eat.

She hadn't run. She hadn't tried to fight me again. She'd just cooked and made snarky comments.

Even after seeing the mess I was—seeing *me*—she sat there, scarred and collared, as if it was nothing.

I lowered my head again, close enough to the plate to inhale the steam. It smelled so damn good, and I was starving. So I ate.

147

Once we had both finished eating, she got up and took both plates to the kitchen before walking into the bathroom without so much as looking back at me, the bloodied clothing a pile on the floor.

I don't beg, I thought as I narrowed my eyes at the heap. Gaining my feet, I shifted into my human form once more. Stubbornness and independence fueled my movements as I stalked to the bathroom, where she poked her head out of the curtain.

Her eyes narrowed as she signed, ***'Bad dog, out.'***

My steps were deliberate as I closed the short distance between the door and the shower. I looked her directly in the eyes, and braced my hand on the shower frame. "I don't beg."

'Good for you, now get out of my shower.'

"How is it that even with a collar on, you manage to be mouthy? Why don't you make your hands more productive and wash me? I need to get this blood off; it's starting to itch."

She didn't respond, instead she just gave me that slow, flat stare of hers and ducked behind the curtain again.

I stepped fully inside, the spray hitting my shoulder as I reached clumsily for the soap. My fingers slipped on the slick bottle, and with only one working hand, I fumbled it twice before catching it against my chest.

She let out an exaggerated sigh, then her hand shot out; she plucked the shampoo from the shelf, flipped the cap with one hand, and slapped a thick glob into my palm.

'You're useless,' she signed with her free hand, then turned her back on me again, like I wasn't even there.

I lathered the soap into my hair, smirking faintly. "Thanks, brat."

She flipped me off, and I chuckled before my eyes caught the large rose tattoo on the top of her shoulder. Tilting my head, I peered closer at it, wiping the soap from my eyes.

She had a fucking bite mark under the tattoo.

"Who the fuck bit you?" I practically growled, trying to control the urge to shift, my wolf enraged that another male had marked *my* female.

She stiffened before turning and signing, *'Your mother.'*

"Don't play with me, Siren. What male had his teeth in your damn skin?"

She rolled her eyes. *'He's dead now, so what does it matter?'*

I swiped more soap from my eyes, the sting helping to clear my head. She wasn't really my female. "Was it someone else you entrapped?"

'I didn't entrap you, dickhead. Hope your eyes burn like hell.'

I growled low in my throat, the sound reverberating off the tile. She didn't flinch, didn't retreat—just stared at me like I was the one bleeding out again.

I wanted to grab her, to shake answers out of her. I wanted to tear the memory of that bite from her skin.

But instead, I stepped back under the water, the spray scorching hot as I tipped my head up into it and scrubbed harder than necessary.

Silence stretched between us, broken only by the hiss of the water and the clench of my jaw.

Chapter 13

Theia...

I sat on the couch in front of the fire I'd started, still feeling raw from the shower, and from him noticing. Jackson was sitting in the recliner with his head back, wearing only a pair of jogging pants.

I hated that he'd noticed the scar under the oleander flower on my shoulder. The whip marks and burns were one thing, but that bite mark was the hardest for me. Petros had left it just a week before I'd ascended into immortality, meaning it had healed just enough to leave an overly defined scar.

I'd chosen the flowers and vines to cover most of my abuse because they were beautiful and deadly, exactly what I wanted to be. Even so, I'd rarely used my Siren's Call to entrap anyone. I was strong and dangerous in my own right, without the help of that magic. That made it even more bitter when Jackson accused me of using it on Petros.

The day I killed him, I felt a surge of power rise in me when he backhanded Theo for stumbling into him. The anger that flooded me was immediate and all-consuming, and I launched myself at him in the tiny sandstone home as Theo cried on the dirt floor.

It was as if something inside me had snapped. Not a break—but a release. My body moved before I could think.

I drove him into the wall so hard that the sandstone cracked behind him. He roared, dazed, and swung at me. I caught his wrist midair. That's when I knew—I was stronger. Faster. Not just angry. Changed. *Immortal.*

I threw him to the floor and didn't stop. I didn't use my voice. I didn't sing. I didn't need the Call. I beat him with the same hands that had once scrubbed his boots and picked stones from his sandals. He tried to crawl away, but I caught him by the back of his tunic and slammed him down again.

When it was done, I stood panting, my hands covered in blood. Theo had gone quiet and wide-eyed, as he crouched in the corner. I knelt beside him, touched his curls, and kissed his cheek.

That was the first time I felt what it meant to be immortal. It wasn't the strength or the speed.

152

It was *freedom*.

The moment I thought no one could hurt us again.

"What are you thinking about over there, brat?"

Jackson's voice pulled me out of the memory with a jolt. When I looked up, his golden eyes were locked on me—even as he remained reclined in the chair.

'How you should put a shirt on.'

"Why? I'm not cold."

I rolled my eyes and snatched the remote off the coffee table, flipping through channels just to give my hands something to do. He leaned his head back again, pretending to ignore me, and I let him—let the TV buzz in the background while the fire cracked and he drifted.

I waited until well after dark before I moved. The quiet had sunk in deep by then and felt heavy. I stood, stretched, and walked to the kitchen.

Time to make something for dinner. Something simple. Something that didn't ask questions or stare at scars.

As I moved around the kitchen, Jackson slipped in and grabbed a beer from the refrigerator and leaned against the counter, watching me. I added some oil to the skillet, ignoring him, and focused on adding the vegetables to the pan to saute. It wasn't like I was able to say anything to him; I had to sign it all.

"Do Sirens have their abilities before they set into immortality?" Jackson asked, causing me to pause and look at him in confusion. "You know, like some demons don't have their powers until they transition or whatever. Lycans can shift after puberty. Then vampires—well, they have a heartbeat until they transition. So, were you able to use your Siren Call before you set into immortality?"

'What does it matter?'

His jaw ticked. "That would be a no, which means you were essentially defenseless when those scars were left all over you."

'They're long dead. Go away.' I turned my back on him and busied myself with cooking again.

"Are you, like, a chef or something? You're always cooking. Everything you make smells fucking amazing."

I let out a gusty sigh. *'Yes, I've been a chef before. I'm old.'*

"I get it, I'll leave you alone," he grumbled and left the kitchen.

Why did I feel bad?

Did I miss him hovering in the kitchen?

Kassie was usually the one with me while I cooked...

Kassie.

154

My eyes burned. I swallowed the pain and fear of the unknown.

The Priestess Jackson spoke to had basically said she was okay, but in that frustrating, cryptic way only Priestesses seem to manage.

My sisters had to be fine. They *had* to be.

I finished cooking and set a plate down for Jackson, although I wasn't sure why I was doing things for him.

We ate in silence, except for him saying, "It's good." I didn't respond. He must've taken the hint because, when it was time for bed, he just nodded to me and shifted into his wolf form, curling up on the floor in front of the door.

Jackson...

Two days had passed since I confronted Theia about her scars.

Two long, quiet days.

Guilt weighed on me. I shouldn't feel bad, not really. But I did.

She'd shut down after that. Not completely, but enough. Short, clipped answers. No emotion. Like talking to a wall I'd built myself.

She moved around the kitchen now, making our third dinner since I'd lost my hand. I sat at the counter, watching. I couldn't help myself—I just loved watching her move.

Yesterday, I even tossed her the game controller just to see her fingers in action. She beat the computer on her first try—no surprise.

I was so completely, stupidly fucked.

The oven door clanged shut, breaking the silence. She turned and leaned against the counter, her eyes on me.

Then her fingers started to move.

'My mother was Teles. She was one of the original Sirens. We were the first daughters. I wonder if that's why she got rid of us when she did—because she didn't know we would set into our immortality years later. We know more and less about Sirens all at the same time. I've had a child, but I've never gotten pregnant again.'

Pain swirled in her eyes as she stared at the seahorse-shaped scar in her palm.

"Why are you telling me this?"

'Boredom.'

"Sirens can only reproduce with immortals. I'm guessing you've never had sex with an immortal since that first

156

pregnancy." The thought of her with anyone else made me uncontrollably jealous.

'He was human. He died with Atlantis.'

"You said *we* were the first daughters. Care to elaborate?"

She bit her lip ring and looked at me. Goddess, I loved it and hated it when she played with that little hoop. *'Our dad was immortal—the first immortal on the island, other than Poseidon, probably. We were separated.'*

"Why do I feel like you're not telling me something?"

'Because I don't want to share details right now.'

"I suppose that is fair."

I leaned forward on the counter, watching her move again. I couldn't help myself. "Why do you keep cooking for me? I kidnapped you. I haven't exactly treated you well."

'I like to cook, and frozen food is trash. It also gives me something to do.' She studied me for a long moment. I felt that gaze in my bones. *'You don't treat me as badly as others have in my life. I understand that you see me as a threat, even if I have no interest in entrapping anyone. It's messy.'*

"How did you learn sign language, anyway?" I changed the subject, unwilling to face the elephant in the room.

I still wasn't sure if I'd kill her or let her live once I'd figured out how to sever the spell.

157

Even after two days of silence—two days of healing and distance—I still wanted her.

Gods, I wanted to touch her.

She gave a small shrug. *'I'm old. I know almost every language there is. Why not learn sign?'*

"You're surprising to me. I thought you would be this manipulative creature. Instead, you're moving around the kitchen, cooking for me, and telling me some heavy shit." I shook my head, looking down at my missing hand. "Then again, you could just be a master manipulator playing the long game."

I looked up to find her pinching the bridge of her nose, frustration etched across her lovely face. When she opened her eyes and looked at me, I almost regretted my words.

'Go chase your tail or something.'

"Why do you always have to start with the damn dog comments?"

'Why do you always have to assume I'm evil? You ripped my throat out and kidnapped me, remember?'

"I didn't rip your throat out," I snarled in response, the image of my pack mate's claws ripping her vocal cords from her throat flooding my mind and filling me with rage. I shouldn't, but I wanted to rip him apart for harming her. I wanted to bring back whoever had left those scars on her just so I could dismember them. I wanted to be bathed in the blood of anyone who ever dared to harm her.

'It won't matter. Once we get the ingredients, you can sever this bond between us and be done. We can go our separate ways—be it the swamp or the grave.'

The silence that hung between us was heavy. Could I do it? Could I kill her when the bond was severed? What would happen if I took her back to the swamp?

"You were alone in the middle of the swamp. The only other creatures I could scent were the Grunch." I tried to work it out. "Why were you there?"

'I told you I was pole dancing,' she signed without emotion.

"Were you looking for the Grunch?" Had she been on a suicide mission when we found her? If that were the case, then why had she entrapped me?

'I was hunting immortal coypu. Eating it helps contain our song,' she signed after a moment. *'I didn't smell the Grunch until just before I heard you. I didn't even have time to react.'*

"You were hunting an animal that dampens your power? But why? Isn't that the only thing you have to protect yourself?"

'I'm stronger than mortals without my song. I've also already told you, I don't entrap males who don't deserve to die.'

"So, I deserve to die?" Anger filled my voice as I tossed the accusation at her.

'No, you don't.'

I just stared at her. She'd told me she never left any alive and that she only entrapped those who deserved to die. Had entrapping me been an accident? An act of necessity from the wolf pack? Had we forced her hand in our pursuit? "You really are going to help me break the bond?"

'I don't really have time to take you on walks, so yes,' she signed with a smirk that both irritated and excited me. That little fucking smirk that made me hard as a rock.

<u>Chapter 14</u>

Theia...

In the days it had taken Jackson to regrow his hand, he hadn't chained me up a single time. We'd spent most of our time playing cards and watching TV. The tension between us had been nearly unbearable, though. Never in my twelve thousand years had I craved a male the way I craved him. I'd even found myself joining him in the shower under the pretense of helping his damaged ass wash, only to end up with his head between my legs. Now that his hand had grown back, that excuse was gone.

Not that it mattered. Now that his hand had grown back, we were on the move again. We'd driven for the better part of the day, until a little after dark, before reaching a bar with a hidden entrance through an alley that appeared to be a dead end. Jackson parked the Jeep before leaning over and slapping cuffs on me.

"Behave in here, brat," he said before getting out of the Jeep.

161

"Dog," I choked out against the shock as he pulled me out of the Jeep and led me by the bouncer. The dark hid the handcuffs he had on me, and the collar kept me mostly silent, but it was obvious he wasn't going to risk leaving me in the car alone. I'd thought we had moved past the cuffs, but apparently that was only within the confines of a safehouse.

He guided me through the bar's door, his hand firm on the small of my back. Once we were inside, he turned to face me, eyes gleaming. "I'm a wolf, unchained, and deadly," he said, tugging on the cuffs at my wrists and pulling me flush against his chest. "You, brat, are the one on a leash. Now, be a good girl and sit down. Maybe, if you behave, I'll let you play later."

Heat coiled low in my stomach, sharp and unwelcome. The fact that his words made me wet pissed me off. I flipped him off and dropped into the nearest seat—because really, what choice did I have?

The bar was strictly immortal with no humans allowed, no safety net. Every single being in here could probably smell exactly what his words had done to me.

Why the fuck did being called "good girl" light me up like that? I shoved the thought aside, locking down the arousal before the scent drew in every horny bastard in the building like flies to honey.

162

Too little, too late. Less than five minutes after I'd sat down, a male came up and looked me over like I'd been looked over all those millennia ago—surveyed like an item to be bought.

"Hey there, Siren. Smells like you're ready to entertain. I didn't know there was going to be an immortal auction tonight."

The smell of cypress and bayberry filled my nose, telling me the fucker invading my personal space was a Bear Shifter. I rolled my eyes at his words and shifted so that I faced away from him.

He leaned even closer, inhaling deeply. "I think I'd enjoy playing with you before I end your miserable existence. No female should have the power you hold, which is probably why you are not only in chains but also have that little collar around your throat."

That did it.

I moved faster than he could track. The cuffs clinked as I spun, and I headbutted him right in the nose. Cartilage cracked, and blood sprayed. He staggered back with a roar, clutching his face.

Without missing a beat, I'd gained my feet and was advancing on the staggering Shifter. Using the cuffs like a weapon, I swung them forward and slammed the metal against his

163

jaw with a satisfying crack. The Bear dropped like a felled log, crashing into a nearby table and shattering it.

The bar fell silent. Every immortal in the room turned to watch. Jackson included.

He stalked toward me, eyes burning, his stance coiled and tense like a predator on the edge of pouncing. The low light of the Edison bulbs threw sharp shadows across his face, casting him in the flickering gold of something dangerous.

I didn't back down.

I lifted my chin and stared him down, daring him to make a move.

"What *the fuck* happened?" he snarled, standing close enough that his body heat rolled over me.

Before I could answer, a new male approached, one who was calm and lean. He smelled of frankincense and myrrh: Vampire.

"If I may," the Vampire said smoothly, his gaze flicking to the crumpled Bear on the floor, "that Grizzly Shifter was trying to get a little too personal. Seems he has an attitude problem." He tilted his head, studying me. "Though I must ask... why is such a lovely Siren in chains?"

"None of your business, Vampire," Jackson growled, his voice low and lethal.

I raised my bound hands and signed sharply, wrists straining against the cuffs. *'He said he was going to play with me before he killed me. You put me in chains, and now everyone thinks I'm for sale.'*

"She's not for sale," Jackson snarled. In a blink, his hand shot out, fisting the Vampire's shirt and yanking him nose to nose.

"Pity," the Vampire murmured, his hands locking around Jackson's wrist. "I hear they taste as sweet as they smell."

Jackson slammed him backward onto the table with bone-rattling force. The air in the bar shifted—everyone watching, no one moving. Then, without hesitation, Jackson drove his hand into the Vampire's chest and ripped out his heart. "She does taste pretty fucking good," he said coldly, holding the lifeless organ in his fist. "Not that you'll ever find out."

Jackson turned to me then. "I got the information we need. Let's go before I decide to remove both of their heads."

He grabbed my elbow and nearly dragged me out of the bar, the bartender yelling at our backs about the bodies. The tension radiating off him was palpable. When we got to the Jeep, he pushed me up against the door and pressed his cheek to mine, his lips brushing against my ear.

"You're a dangerous little brat, aren't you? I'd like to know how the fuck you managed to knock out a Bear Shifter almost as badly as I want to fuck you against this Jeep."

I turned my head, met his heat with my own, and ran my tongue slowly and deliberately up the side of his cheek.

Jackson stilled, a low growl vibrating from his chest as it pressed against mine. His hands flexed against the door like he was debating whether to grip or destroy.

My smile curled slowly and wickedly as I looked up into his molten gaze.

His jaw ticked. "Careful, brat."

I leaned in, lips grazing the edge of his jaw. "Always," I choked out against the shock of the collar.

He slammed a palm beside my head, and for a second I thought he might kiss me, or strangle me. Possibly both.

Instead, he exhaled through his nose, sharp and frustrated. "Get in the Jeep before I bend you over the hood and spank that bratty ass of yours."

I laughed low in my throat, earning myself a healthy shock, and signed, *'Promises, promises.'*

Jackson yanked the passenger door open with more force than necessary. I slid inside without another word, the ghost of his heat still clinging to my skin.

166

He circled the hood slowly, like he needed the walk to calm the monster I'd stirred in him. When he finally climbed into the driver's seat, the air inside the Jeep felt like a powder keg—one spark away from igniting.

He didn't say a word as he drove out of the parking lot and set off down the dark road, but the tension crackled loud enough to drown out everything else.

Three hours later, Jackson parked the car next to a stream that fed into one of the lakes and got out. He ran his hand through his hair as he looked at me, still sitting in the passenger seat. All this time, he still hadn't uncuffed me. I rolled my eyes and looked away from him. The next thing I knew, he was opening my door. "Come on. I can't leave you here. Just stay back and stay quiet. The lakes are dangerous, but I need the weeping water to fix this shit."

There he went again, accusing me of entrapping him when I had not hummed a single fucking note. All because I made his dick hard.

Getting out of the car, I shoulder-checked him—knocking him flat on his ass—before walking straight to the stream. With a hop, I jumped into the shallow water and began kicking my feet, mocking him in my own way.

"Are you fucking crazy? Get out of the damn water!" he snarled, stalking toward me.

He'd made it only two steps before I was covered in a cold, wet embrace. "Sssuch sssorrow," a gurgly, haunted voice said in my ear. I could feel my heart breaking all over again, the pain of Theo flooding me. Tears began to stream down my face; a sob ripped from my body. The pain of his loss was so powerful that I didn't notice whether the collar shocked me or not.

"I can tassste your sssorrow."

The pain of the spear ripped through my chest and protruded from his tiny body. The soul-wrenching agony filled every fiber of my being. In that moment, I wanted to drown—wanted to let the creature suck me under, where I would live in that sorrow forever, just as my son was gone forever. I wanted to feel the burn of the water filling my lungs as they struggled for oxygen, over and over again, in the never-ending misery that was this loss.

"Let her go!" Jackson bellowed, trying to get to me, but the water kept pushing him back onto the shore of the small stream.

"I know your pain, I am made from your pain," the creature said in my ear. "What do you want with thisss broken Sssiren?" The creature directed its question at Jackson as my sobs

168

died down, wiping away my tears with its watery form—the cool touch of the water both soothing and excruciating at the same time.

"I'm bound to her, I need your water to break the curse," he snarled, his anger evident as he stood at the water's edge, dripping wet from being thrown back by the creature. He didn't want me; he wanted to be *free* of me.

"Do you want to leave with him or ssstay with me?" the creature asked, the odd pressure of the water loosening from my body. Thoughts of my sisters at the gates of Atlantis flickered in my mind. Jackson's teasing smile when we played games flashed in my mind, along with the conflict that often filled his eyes.

Before I could respond, Jackson was there, pulling me away from the creature and shoving me behind him. He bared his teeth at the creature, even as the thought that they still needed me settled in. "She's not staying with you."

"Ssshe has given me some of her sssorrow. I will give you sssome of my water."

Without thought or hesitation, I threw myself in front of him, tears still streaming down my face. "No!" The shock that shot through my body made my cold knees want to buckle; my body felt brittle and broken from the loss all over again. Somehow, deep in the pits of my very being, I knew that this

169

creature was offering not simply to give him the water; it was going to fill his lungs and drag him beneath the water's surface. "No more sorrow," I choked out against the shock. Jackson grabbed me and pulled me back into his body.

"You are covered in my sssorrow, Sssiren. You will return to me," the creature hissed as it splashed into the stream, disappearing as if it had never been there.

Before I knew what was going on, Jackson was dragging me out of the water and back to the Jeep. "What the fuck just happened?" he demanded, looking me over like he actually gave a fuck. I shoved his hands away from me as best I could with my cuffed wrists. "Did that thing hurt you? That creature is said to drag immortals to the bottom of the lakes and drown them over and over again. The ones who make it out live as broken shells of themselves for the rest of eternity."

A snort left me in response to what he'd said. My sisters and I were already little more than shells. Had they not been there that day, had Poseidon not put Theo back into my hand, I would have found a way to end my existence after watching Atlantis burn. My cuffed hands lifted my shirt away from my body, and I squeezed the fabric, pointedly looking at him. "Sorrow." I choked out again, surprised that he hadn't figured it out.

170

His eyes widened, and he pulled a jar out of his pocket that had three vials inside it. "Squeeze," he commanded as he held the first vial up to my shirt.

<u>Chapter 15</u>

Jackson...

After filling the vials with water, I retrieved dry clothing from the duffel and made her change.

She'd put herself between me and the creature. I'd felt her pain—felt her heart breaking in my own chest—as the monster washed away her tears, feeding off her. And still, she'd put herself between me and the creature. It had to be a game, right? But what could she possibly gain from it?

She could have attacked me when the Gorgon took my hand and used my thumbprint to free herself, but she hadn't. She'd demanded the keys and ordered directions on the GPS. Why was she working with me to sever the connection? Was it because I wasn't fully entrapped?

Getting in the Jeep, I cranked the heat to full blast and glanced over to see her shivering, curled into the door. She was

172

staring at her palm again. The pain radiating from her felt like a physical entity.

"When we get to the next safehouse, you should take a bath—try to warm yourself up." I didn't know what else to say. My instincts screamed at me to wrap her in my arms and comfort her, but my training warned against it. Not that training had stopped me from touching her. Or tasting her.

Goddess, help me. I was in way over my head.

We drove in silence to the closest safehouse, and when we got inside, she turned to me and fisted her hands in my shirt just before her lips locked on mine. I staggered back into the wall, dropped the duffel, and pulled her with me. A silent sob escaped her lips and broke the kiss. I placed my hands on her shoulders and gently pushed her back.

"Go take a bath. You'll feel better."

Her jaw clenched, and tears welled in her eyes, but she stepped away from me. Watching her walk to the bathroom, when all I wanted to do was pull her back into my arms, was an agony I hadn't expected. A hollow ache filled my chest, and my throat tightened as I watched the door close.

I took a steadying breath and tossed my phone on the counter before putting the duffel in the bedroom. *She's the enemy.*

I had to keep reminding myself of that, no matter how sweet her face looked or how her tears made my chest tighten.

My phone buzzed on the counter, and I went to check my message. To my surprise, it was a text from the Priestess, but not the kind I'd expected.

`Lycan, you are being followed. Here is the address of an Oracle who will trade vehicles with you and use a glamor spell to look like you and your musical companion. He will need the Phoenix alive. You have a few days to switch. P.S. A ball gag will keep her from singing as well, unless you like shocking her while your head is between her legs.`

The following text that came through was an address, and I felt my face burn slightly. I glanced at the bathroom door, glad Theia couldn't see my face. The fact that the Priestess knew wasn't entirely surprising. That didn't mean I liked her knowing. I was trying to get her to lift the damn enchantment the Siren had me under, after all.

Someone was following us. I had to wonder how far behind they were. Was it someone from my pack? Had we drawn attention from one of the stops we'd made, looking for the items the Priestess wanted? Was there someone trying to rescue Theia?

I locked the phone screen and walked to the fridge. We had a couple of days, so we would stay the night here, then head out in the morning. I had no idea how long it would take to get the Phoenix, but that was a problem for the morning.

Opening our cooler, I unpacked what little food we had left and looked at the alcohol. The Creature of Weeping Water had done a number on Theia. I picked up the bottle of tequila I'd bought just yesterday and headed for the bathroom. I hesitated only a moment at the door before entering.

Her head tilted to the side, and she glared at me through red-rimmed eyes before signing, *'What do you want?'*

"I brought tequila." I walked over and handed her the bottle. Her large eyes looked up at me in shock before she took a drink and leaned her head back.

I sank down next to the tub with my back to her to keep myself from looking. Goddess, did I want to look. I'd looked at her so many times before, and it was never enough. The touch she allowed was never enough. I wanted all over her, all of the time.

Refocusing myself, I decided to break the silence. "I just got a text with our next location. We'll stay the night here, then get going first thing in the morning."

175

I heard the water slosh before her wet arm draped over my shoulder. The clink of the bottle sounded as she set it down next to me, and her lips feathered over the back of my neck. She began pulling my damp shirt up, and I tilted my head back, her lips moving to the side of my neck.

"What are you doing, brat?"

Her teeth rasped over my shoulder before her distorted voice came into my ear. "Touching."

Goddess, I wanted to take that damn collar off, wanted to hear her voice without it causing her pain. "Don't play with me, brat, or I might just get in that bath with you." I wanted her so bad, I couldn't stand it.

Her only answer was the slow drag of her tongue up the side of my neck. A groan escaped my lips. The sound of more water sloshing filled the room before both her arms wrapped around me, pulling my shirt over my head. I could feel my body shaking with need as I twisted around and looked down at the female in the tub, the water hiding nothing.

She pulled the plug and stood, water cascading down her naked form. I raked my eyes over her tattoos and piercings. I'd had each of them in my mouth—from her lip ring to her nipples. Her hood piercing was probably my favorite. That was the one I wanted to touch now, the one that would make her come apart with just a few flicks of my tongue.

'I still only want touch, but I want to touch you.' She chewed her lip ring as her eyes scanned my exposed chest.

My lips quivered, and my erection throbbed. "Tit for tat." If she wanted to touch me, I wasn't going to stop her, but my face would be between her legs while she did.

'Towel, dog. Before I change my mind.'

A low growl rumbled in my chest as I grabbed a towel from the towel rack and stalked toward her. "I'll fucking dry you off, brat."

I wrapped the towel around her and pulled her into my body, my lips locking on hers in a punishing kiss. We stumbled back into the wall, her wet body pressed to mine, the towel doing little as the threads of my restraint vanished. Her legs wrapped around me, my hands cupping her ass as I pinned her to the damn wall.

My hand traveled up and fisted in her hair, yanking her head back so that I could have better access to her throat. The fucking collar was in my damn way. I snarled and pressed my lips to her ear. "Do you have any idea how bad I want to fuck you right here against this wall?"

I ground myself between her legs, my pants the only thing between us. The thought that all I had to do was unbutton my jeans and I could bury myself in her was so tempting.

"Taste—you," she rasped out, the jolt of the collar tingling into my own skin at her words.

"Fuck," I breathed, then turned from the wall, readjusting my hold and packing her out of the bathroom. Our lips rejoined as I stumbled into the bedroom and tossed her on the bed. It took only seconds for me to kick off my boots and strip my pants. I was climbing over top of her in the next breath, our lips locked once more.

She locked one hand in my hair, the other slid down and wrapped around my cock.

"Tighter," I snarled against her lips.

She obeyed, and I pumped my hips into her fist as our tongues dueled, her other hand fisted, tight enough in my hair to be nearly painful.

I allowed myself that little pleasure for only a few moments before I rolled, pulling her on top of me. I could feel the heat of her so close that it was beyond tempting to plunge myself inside of her, but she'd said *touch only*.

"Turn around, let me fuck you with my tongue," I demanded instead. She'd said touch only, so I would settle for that. I'd plunge my tongue inside her and rake my teeth over her clit, tormenting that little hood piercing until she came over and over again. If she wanted to taste me, then I'd fuck her throat and watch her cheeks flush when I reminded her that it could be her sweet little cunt I was buried in instead.

She'd readjusted in moments, her knees on either side of my head. My hands cupped the cheeks of her ass and urged her down while my head came up off the mattress. At the same time, I'd dragged my tongue over her slit, and her hand had fisted around me again, drawing my erection to her lips.

I groaned against her core as her lips wrapped around me, her tongue circling just under the head. Her teeth rasped over my shaft, and my hips jerked up, thrusting deeper into her mouth.

Her head bobbed up and down while her fist pumped below her lips. I pulled her hips down closer, burying my face in her as we both lost control. I tried to hold back my release, tried to savor the feel of her mouth around my cock and the taste of her on my tongue. Her head bobbed, her fist tightened, and I lost it.

She began swallowing, her breathing increasing, as I came deep in her throat. Her nails rasped on my thigh, and her own legs began to shake, and a whimper escaped her lips, sending a jolt through both of us as she hurried to pull her mouth away from my cock.

"Fuck," I rasped as I jerked at the sudden sensation. I grabbed her ass cheeks and pulled her down onto my face. "I'm not done," I snarled into her.

"Jacks—" she choked out, her hands gripping my legs as I continued flicking that wicked little piercing and sucking on her until she completely shattered. I delved my tongue inside her and reveled in the way her core clenched around me, seeking more.

I finally let her go, and she collapsed to the side, panting.

"Good girl," I panted, lying back with my eyes closed and my chest heaving. Never in a million years would I have thought getting my shit shocked could intensify an orgasm.

She lay there boneless beside me, her breath still uneven. I ran my hand slowly down her spine. She shivered and turned so that she was lying with her head next to mine, a satisfied smile playing on her lips. I tugged her close, tucking her to my chest. "You need rest, brat."

She stiffened for a moment before relaxing. A part of me was panicking at what I was doing—letting her sleep with me. Another part of me was too content to give a damn. The memory of her tears still tightened my chest, not to mention the fear I'd felt when the creature had held her in its watery grasp.

I knew that fear was twofold. The bond between us caused it, but the logical part of me feared what would have happened

180

had she been taken. Would I have gone mad? Would I have been freed from her entrapment? I wasn't fully entrapped, after all—I was still aware.

I glanced at her now, her head resting on my chest and her arms curled around herself. How could someone so small and delicate be so deadly? She was helping me. She'd told me and shown me she was helping. She must have entrapped me by accident and was now trying to make it right.

Maybe she wasn't a monster after all.

Chapter 16

Theia…

Morning came, and I found myself tucked against Jackson's warm side. We were both still naked from last night's events. I lifted my head from his chest and sat up, looking around the room for the duffel. Spotting it, I got out of bed and went over to get clothing, leaving Jackson sound asleep.

As I got dressed, I tried to remember the last time I'd done anything like that with a male. Maybe a hundred years ago—maybe longer. I'd had plenty of mouths between my legs, male and female alike; the itch demanded satisfaction. But giving back to a male in bed? That was *rare*. Full-blown sex with a male had never really been an option for me. Not that it ruled out the occasional strap-on… or other toys.

182

"Toss me some pants, would you?" Jackson's voice startled me out of my thoughts. I turned to see him grinning, his arms folded behind his head.

'Someone looks pleased with themself,' I signed before pulling out pants and tossing them at him.

"If it had been your pussy I was fucking last night instead of your mouth, you would be having trouble walking today."

I stared at him for a moment before shrugging and walking out of the bedroom, knowing it would piss him off more than he'd just pissed me off. Hell, if I were being honest, he'd actually turned me on just a little. Why was I still so fucking attracted to him? Did the Lycan mate bond work both ways or something?

I began setting up the coffee pot, pushing down my desire to let the Lycan make good on his word. Opening the bag of grounds, I let the robust aroma fill my senses.

My sisters still needed me. That thought had been part of what had anchored me yesterday. Jackson only needed me because of the bond. He thought I'd entrapped him. Why did that hurt so bad? I didn't want to be tied to him. I didn't have time for a mate.

"You better be making enough for me too, brat," Jackson said as he came up behind me, brushed my hair away from my

183

face, and ran his nose over the side of my throat. "Goddess, you smell good, you know that? Like hibiscus and blood orange."

I turned around and gave him a what-the-fuck look before pressing start on the coffee pot and going to the counter to sit and wait. Had sucking his cock been enough to cause a whole-ass personality swap? I glanced at him as he pulled a carton of eggs out of the fridge.

Was he making me breakfast?

"After breakfast, we need to get going; we have a lot of ground to cover to reach this next address."

'Where to this time?' I signed as my eyes roamed over his body. Part of me, the one that recognized the distraction, wanted him to cover up. But another, far more compelling part, relished the raw, unadulterated view, finding a delicious warmth spread through me at the sight.

"The address is in Wyoming. It should take us most of the day to get there." He cracked a few eggs into a bowl before continuing. "We only have a few items left, and the Priestess will have what she needs."

'That's good. Are the rest of the ingredients going to be hard to get?' I didn't know what else to sign. I couldn't explain the feelings swirling inside me either. If I had to guess, the

184

encounter with the Creature of Weeping Water had left my emotions scrambled and easily misled.

"That's yet to be determined." He turned away from me then and shifted his focus to making what I assumed were omelets.

The rest of the morning was silent as we ate and packed everything into the Jeep. Jackson turned the radio on, and we drove for hours down the highway, the sound of punk rock and heavy metal filling the silence. I approved of his taste in music.

I leaned my head against the window, not really even seeing the world beyond. My thoughts swirled around my sisters and how I'd been so willing just to let go and allow my life to end. Yes, I missed Theo, but could I inflict more pain upon my sisters by leaving them? Was there a way for me to talk Jackson out of killing me? What would that take?

Jackson...

We'd stopped twice all day to eat and stretch before we finally reached the address I'd been given. The driveway had been long and winding, gravel crunching beneath the tires as we climbed higher into the hills of Wyoming. Frost clung to the edges of the worn path, and patches of light snow held stubbornly to the shaded spots beneath pine trees. The air was thin and sharp,

185

the kind of cold that bit through your clothes without mercy. At the end of the drive sat a small, weathered cabin, its wood darkened by years of wind and winter. An extended-cab green truck was parked out front, and a smallish male sat on the steps drinking from a thermos, his breath frosting the air.

"Stay here," I ordered Theia, not taking my eyes off the male. I got out of the Jeep, and the male looked up at me, his gaze unsettlingly focused.

"My sister sent you the terms but probably failed to give instructions," the male said, looking up at me with a half grin.

"The Priestess is your sister?" I countered, catching his scent of hazelnut coffee—an Oracle.

He stood and stretched before rummaging in his coat pocket and pulling out a set of keys. "I'll give you the instructions later. You can't go until morning anyway." He nodded toward the Jeep then. "Why don't you have her get out and stretch her legs?"

Crossing my arms, I sized up the male in front of me. "Why did you get your keys out?"

"My sister just told me today that you were coming. I'll need to get some items to make this little decoy convincing, but I wanted to ensure I was here when you arrived. It would do you no good to find an empty cabin." He tilted his head, stretching to see Theia through the window.

A low growl rumbled in my chest in warning. I may be trying to sever the bond, but she was still *mine*.

The male chuckled. "You can calm down. You're more my type than she is, if you catch my drift. Don't worry, I can tell when a male isn't interested."

"Then why are you trying so hard to look at her?" I demanded, my hackles still raised.

"I'll need to conjure a convincing decoy, and for that, I need to get a good look at both of you, at least from the waist up." He glanced back at me and looked me up and down.

The sound of the Jeep door slamming pulled my attention away from the male. Theia stepped out in the light winter jacket I'd bought her, her boots landing with a crunch on the gravel, her breath puffing in the frigid air.

I made a mental note to get us both better winter gear now that we were farther north.

'Please tell me you know ASL,' she addressed the male.

"I'm guessing that collar around your throat is why you're signing things to me. Unfortunately, I don't know how to sign. My name is Marcus."

"She's a Siren. The collar is a necessary precaution," I grumbled. Why the fuck did I care that he was talking to her?

187

"If you say so. Seeing as you're the one talking for her, do you think you could introduce me to the pretty little daughter of Ares?"

My head whipped toward Theia, who shrugged. "Daughter of *Ares*? You are the daughter of the Greek God of war?"

'You didn't ask. He did ask my name. Now, be a good dog and speak.'

My jaw twitched at her snarky comment. "I call her brat." Two could play her little game.

"Somehow I feel like if I call her that, she may take my testicles, collar or no collar," Marcus said as he looked me up and down again, as if assessing my sanity.

Theia snapped her fingers, drawing my attention back to her. *'He's right, and tell him to get popcorn so we can both look at you like that. You are a sexy show dog.'*

"Theia. Her fucking name is Theia, and she's a pain in the *ass*."

'You like my ass.' She wiggled her eyebrows at me before heading for the porch where Marcus still stood. She stepped up next to the male, and her eyes flicked between me and him.

Biting her bottom lip, she nodded at the male, then held her hands out in front of her, palms facing each other, and slowly

188

moved them farther apart until Marcus gave a low whistle. She shot me a wicked grin and wiggled her eyebrows, just to drive the point home.

My cock wanted to harden at her smug look, but the growl that came out of me was pure warning. She was playing games she didn't understand. Or maybe she understood too well. "Are you trying to die today?"

Theia just shrugged innocently, hands now behind her back like she hadn't just casually broadcast my dick size like a weather report.

Marcus shook his head. "The cabin is unlocked. Go on inside and make yourselves at home while I go get some things from town. There is a roast in the slow cooker."

Grabbing the duffle from the Jeep, Theia and I went inside the cabin. I wasn't sure what I was going to do with her and didn't know if I could trust the male, but what choice did I have?

When we got inside, I watched as the Oracle pulled out of the driveway and then turned to Theia. "Why are you such a pain in the ass? Things would be so much easier if you would just behave."

She gave me a sideways glance before sighing. *'Before I set into my immortality, I was a slave for ten years. I didn't let him break me; why would I let you?'*

189

Her confession left me stunned. Suddenly, the scars covered by her tattoos made sense. I was filled with rage and guilt all at the same time. "I'm not trying to break you." It was all I had, all I could say.

'Besides, you like my ass,' she signed again, a cheeky grin plastered across her face.

I shook my head and dropped the duffle next to the couch before heading to the kitchen. The cabin was an open space with a set of steps and a door tucked away on the far wall. "Let's eat; I'm hungry."

There was a deck of cards on the counter in the kitchen, as well as bowls and silverware next to the slow cooker. Apparently, the Oracle had been thoughtful enough to provide entertainment while he disappeared.

We'd eaten and played different card games until Marcus returned. Theia had gone to take a shower while the Oracle gave me the location and instructions on how to retrieve the Phoenix.

First thing in the morning, we were going to Devils Tower.

Theia...

Jackson dragged me to the base of the great structure before the sun had even risen. Marcus went into town and

190

returned with climbing gear and winter clothing. The thick work gloves were a blessing, not just for protection against the cold, but also because they provided a better grip on the rock as I climbed.

Together, we scaled Devils Tower in search of the next ingredient on his list. The wind bit at my exposed cheeks, though the sock hat did a decent job of keeping my ears warm. Marcus had said we should count ourselves lucky that it had been a mild winter so far. But that hadn't stopped ice from forming in the rock's narrow crevices, making every foothold a gamble and every handhold slick with danger.

We cleared the top, and Jackson pulled me up, allowing me to gain my feet easily. There, nestled in its nest of twigs, was the most beautiful bird I'd ever seen. Red, blue, and gold feathers glinted in the first rays of sunlight. The phoenix lifted its head and looked at us.

"I'm not going to hurt you; I just need your help." Jackson's voice was gentle as he held up his hands to the bird.

It looked at me, its beautiful eyes holding an undeniable intelligence.

"Please," I mouthed, hoping it wouldn't fly away. The sooner Jackson got all the ingredients for the stupid spell, the sooner he would find out I hadn't entrapped him and wasn't the

evil creature his kind thought I was. I just wanted to return to my sisters and be done with him.

"I need your help with ingredients for a spell. I don't want to hurt you. I need feathers," Jackson reasoned with the bird. It looked away from us, at the rising sun, then down at its nest.

It stood, its long tail feathers resembling those of a resplendent quetzal. I mentally thanked Kassie for her bird obsession years ago. The bird lifted its head from its nest, a bundle of feathers in its beak. It hopped out of the nest and walked calmly toward us before setting the feathers on the ground in front of Jackson.

It looked like he wouldn't need the bag he'd brought to catch and pluck the poor thing.

It turned its head and looked back at the morning light. Before the stunning bird could take another step, Jackson had forced the bag over its body and tossed it over his back. "Sorry, but I have to give you to the Oracle."

"Stop!"

ZAP.

Why was he taking the bird? It had given him the feathers he needed!

"Shut up so you don't hurt yourself, and pick up the feathers. I don't want to hurt the bird by plucking her."

192

My mouth hung open like an idiot as I looked at him. He didn't want to hurt the bird, and yet he'd shoved it into a sack after it had given him what he'd fucking needed for the damn spell! I snatched up the feathers and flipped him off. "Kidnapper," I choked out against the zap. First me, and now the bird!

"I told you to fucking stop talking."

"Let—" *zap* "bird—" *zap,* "go." *Zap.*

"Don't you fucking get it? I can't! Because of you! Because you are a fucking Siren! Do you think I want to take this creature's freedom away? I don't, but it's the price I have to pay, thanks to you!"

Shaking my head, I shoved past him and tucked the feathers into my bra so they wouldn't fall out on the climb down. I was half fucking tempted just to jump and let the fucker pack both me and the bird.

Chapter 17

Theia...

The climb down had been even worse than the climb up Devils Tower for more reasons than one. When we got in the Jeep, Jackson gently handed the bird to me. "Be careful with it."

I simply narrowed my eyes at him. To my surprise, the Phoenix was not fighting. The urge to fling open my door and release it was almost too strong to ignore as I stared at the brown material.

"We need to get the Phoenix to the Oracle unharmed. He said it's important to her survival because of her feathers being used in the spell," Jackson explained as he started up the Jeep.

I glanced at him, then back at the bird in my lap. He was hell-bent on severing the bond. He refused to believe that I hadn't entrapped him. It wasn't my fault that this bird was involved, but I still felt a twinge of guilt as we drove back to the cabin.

We got back to the cabin and entered with the Phoenix still in the bag, only to find Marcus in the living room filling up a fucking blow-up doll!

"Oh! Shut the door and let her out of that bag, it can't be comfortable," Marcus said as he continued pumping the handheld air pump.

"What the hell are you doing?" Jackson demanded as I released the Phoenix into the room and watched as she flew off to sit on the back of the couch and glared at us.

"Preparing the decoy. Amani is going to help me bring her to life. I'll need to dress her, of course, with something Theia has worn."

"You named the blow-up doll Amani?" Jackson asked, glancing at me.

"Don't be ridiculous. The doll is named Victoria. You know, because she's got secrets," Marcus said with a smile as he finished filling the doll.

'He's replacing me with a blow-up doll and a dad joke. Are you fucking kidding?' I signed.

Jackson shook his head at my comment, then looked back at Marcus. "Cute, but who is Amani?"

"The Phoenix. Her name is Amani."

195

The bird flew over to him and landed on the floor, inspecting the blow-up doll before turning to look at us again.

"There is some food on the counter for you, Amani, if you're hungry. Just some peas and tuna. I wasn't sure what you liked, but I'm sure it's better than bugs," Marcus spoke to the Phoenix like she could understand him.

To my surprise, she went to the counter and began eating both.

"Alright. I'll be leaving as soon as Amani is done eating. I've got a cage for her to keep her safe during the trip, if she's willing to get inside it. I'm really hoping she's as agreeable as she seems now, but without being able to talk to her, all I've been able to determine is her name."

"Fascinating. Can I get your truck keys now? I'd like to start on the last item your sister gave me."

Marcus stood and walked to the counter, where he dropped a set of keys. "I'd recommend waiting a day or two to leave so the cameras show the Jeep and no trace of the two of you. I'm guessing that's why she told me to do this."

"Thanks for the advice," Jackson grumbled before moving to the couch and flopping down. "Come sit down, brat; I know you're probably sore and cold from our little outing."

'Go to hell,' I signed, not wanting to sit with him.

196

He sighed heavily before getting up and stalking toward me, then leaning down, placing his mouth next to my ear. "Every day that I'm with you and can't have you—beneath me, on top of me, around me—is *hell*. Every time your voice is cut off by that collar, I'm forced to keep on you because you could entrap me further; it's *hell*. Every fucking part of me craves you."

With that, he walked to the kitchen. He left me standing there feeling a mix of shock and arousal. My core clenched, and my skin prickled in anticipation of his touch on my skin.

"Do you have any alcohol?"

"There is a case of beer in the fridge, a bottle of vodka, some rum, a case of mixed drinks, and a bottle of tequila in the freezer. There is also a little bourbon left in the cabinet above the stove." Marcus began dressing the doll in what appeared to be my clothing.

About twenty minutes later, Marcus had left with the Phoenix, who calmly got in the cage, with him promising to explain on the road. After they left, Jackson and I were alone in the quiet of the cabin.

Jackson opened the freezer and pulled out the bottle of Patrón before walking over to me. "Look, I know I pissed you off by taking the bird, and I was kinda a dick to you about doing it.

197

So, just have a drink and let's move on. It's not like either of us can change this shit now."

I just stared at him as he sat down on the couch and leaned his head back, staring at the ceiling. "The next thing we need is some candles made from Oger's earwax. There is a place in Idaho to get those, so that's going to be a long trip."

I snatched the bottle off the table and took a healthy swig. I didn't give a fuck that it was still early in the day, and apparently, neither did he.

The last item. I had to wonder how long I had to find a way out of this. I couldn't run, not with the collar on. I swallowed convulsively before kicking my shoes off, pulling my feet up onto the couch, and leaning sideways against the back.

Jackson glanced at me and put his hand on one of my feet. "If you are bored, you can watch TV or something."

I reached for the remote and did what he'd suggested, needing the distraction more than anything. I began flipping through channels until I found some old CSI reruns and settled on that. Jackson's hand was gently rubbing my foot as he stared blankly at the screen. I wasn't sure he even realized he was doing it, but the contact was comforting somehow, so I didn't stop him.

A few hours later, and after a lot of alcohol, I found myself lying with my head in his lap as we watched TV. He was stroking my hair when he finally broke the silence. "If I keep you, they'll kill us both." I shifted, shocked by his words, and looked up at him. "I know it's just because you've entrapped me, but I still want to keep you; my instincts crave you."

'Just let me go then. I'll keep helping you and not fight any of the things that need to be done to sever this bond.'

"Such a pretty little danger. If I let you go, how do I know you won't entrap someone else?" His words were slurred from the alcohol, and his expression held a vulnerability I'd not seen before.

'I don't have any reason to. I also avoid Lycans. Your kind is safe from me.' I wanted so badly to tell him again that I hadn't entrapped him, but if I did, would he believe me and realize the mate bond was real? What would happen if he did?

"What would happen if I just gave in? If I just took the collar off and let you fully entrap me, would I still feel this conflict?"

'You're drunk. Just watch TV.' I wasn't sure if talking about it was a good idea or not. We were both drunk; the empty tequila bottle was proof of that, along with the multitude of empty beer cans on the coffee table.

"You're right. I shouldn't have said that. It confuses me when you're not a brat."

199

His head fell back again, and his eyes closed, but his fingers kept playing in my hair. When he said "they," was he talking about his pack? If he did just let me go, would his pack hunt me down? Would I be putting my sisters in danger if I did find a way to live?

As the day wore on, I'd cooked us something to eat, and we'd continued drinking before falling asleep on the couch. At some point, I'd ended up lying on top of him, my head on his stomach and my body between his legs. I was warm and content, surrounded by his smell, even if the thought that he had to kill me for the sake of his pack still nagged at the back of my mind.

Chapter 18

Jackson…

I woke to a comforting, warm weight on top of me and looked to see that Theia was sound asleep. When had we ended up in this position? My head was foggy as I glanced around. We were still on the couch. Dirty dishes and empty alcohol containers littered the coffee table.

Goddess, we'd drunk enough to kill a mortal.

I should make her move. I should be disgusted that a Siren was using me as her pillow. Instead, I inhaled her scent—that sweet mix of blood orange and hibiscus, the very flower she hated. I reached forward and brushed her hair from her face, intending to catch a glimpse of her sleeping, but her eyes opened, and she sat up immediately, looking around in surprise.

She rubbed her eyes and glared at me. *'I need coffee.'*

201

"Why are you glaring at me? You're the one who slept on top of me all night," I demanded as she got to her feet.

She arched her brow before signing, *'Every time I tried to move, you growled at me and held me down. I think you thought I was a chew toy someone was trying to take from you.'*

I rubbed my face and let out a gust of breath. "Why do you have to start first thing in the morning?" I looked at her for a response, only to have her wink at me. She was fucking teasing me. "You're such a brat." I pushed myself up into a sitting position and picked up my phone to see if I'd gotten any messages.

Sure enough, there was a message from the Priestess.

I forgot to mention that the candle wicks need to be made from Agropelter hair. They are nasty little things, but you and the Siren should be able to handle them.

A heavy sigh escaped me at the prospect of yet another task. Looking at the female making coffee in the kitchen, I couldn't help but wonder how much longer I would be trapped under her spell and yearning for her. Once the spell was broken, would I still feel an attraction to her? Did I genuinely like her personality?

202

'Staring at me won't make it brew any faster,' she signed from the kitchen.

"Apparently, we need Agropelter fur to make the candlewick on the candles we need." I rubbed the back of my head and waited for her response.

'When do we leave? Marcus said to wait a day or two, but we have our next objective.'

"We will head out later today. It will take us a couple of days to even get there."

***

It had taken us two full days to reach Oregon. We'd parked outside of Umatilla National Forest, leaving the truck on the side of a road that wasn't heavily traveled.

The snow was heavy and loud beneath our boots, and I hated it. Not for the cold. I ran hot, but for the way it dampened my senses. Every step crackled in my sensitive ears, and each gust threw scents off course.

We'd been tracking the Agropelters for three days. The telltale signs were there: stripped branches high in the canopy, sharpened sticks jammed into tree bark like warnings, and a stench that reminded me of burnt sap and urine.

The wiry cryptids were notorious for being volatile, seeking out opportunities to hurl sticks with deadly precision, a

203

reputation that had me on edge and listening for them. More often than not, they didn't target humans, but with Immortals, it was like they enjoyed watching us die and come back when a stick was rammed through the eye socket or a branch through the chest cavity.

Theia walked behind me, her long coat tight at the waist, her hair tangled with melting snowflakes. She hadn't tried to speak in the last two days. The collar was doing its job, but I was starting to hate the silence.

She tapped my shoulder and pointed up. A shadow flitted between the branches.

I nodded and crouched low for a new angle. "They're close."

The moment the words left my mouth, a splintered log the size of my arm flew from above and slammed into the tree beside me. Bark exploded, and I swore as I dove to the side.

Theia didn't flinch as she stepped behind a rock and crouched, her eyes scanning the trees with eerie calm.

I growled, sniffing the air. "Come down here, you little fuckers."

Another branch hurled down, then a second, then seven more.

One clipped Theia's shoulder, and she hissed through her teeth but stayed upright even as my blood boiled with rage that she'd been hit. Her eyes narrowed, and she grabbed a chunk of ice and flung it upward at the trees in one smooth throw.

A high-pitched screech answered her.

"You pissed it off," I snapped, wishing she would find a new spot instead of the half-crouch behind the fucking boulder.

She turned to me with a dry, almost amused look as if to say, *"Good."*

From the trees above, the Agropelters began hooting and clattering, like unhinged woodpeckers on shrooms. One dropped down just long enough to flash gnarled fingers and a twisted, vine-cloaked face.

I lunged for it. The creature shrieked and scrambled back up, but not before I was able to snatch a tuft of greasy fur.

Another dive-bomber came swinging down from the trees, and Theia side-stepped its assault before spinning and kicking it mid-chest with her dainty booted foot. The creature flopped into the snow, stunned from the impact.

I scooped up more fur while it writhed, and she threw a rock into the canopy to keep the rest back. For a second, our eyes met, and I could tell she felt alive from the action, her cheeks flushed with cold.

205

'Do we have enough?' she signed.

I let go of the Agropelter that had just regained its senses. "Yeah, let's go before they start again."

Before we could move, another stick was launched, this time going clean through her shoulder. She let out a strangled cry that was a mix of pain and rage.

"Theia!" I reached for her, but she was already spinning to face the direction the stick had come from.

She ripped it from her body and launched it into the trees at a fleeing Agropelter. To my surprise, it went through the thing's back, and it fell to the ground with a single cry of pain.

The chittering that had filled the snowy forest only moments ago fell silent. "We're leaving now," I said, my hackles raised. Without giving her a chance to respond or even move, I tossed her over my shoulder and began running through the trees, calling on my Lycan strength to propel me forward so fast the trees were an impossible blur.

As we neared the road where the truck was parked, I finally slowed down. I let Theia slide down my body until her feet met the snow with a soft crunch.

"Let me see your shoulder," I said, reaching for her, only to have her punch me in the shoulder hard enough to knock me off balance for a moment. "What the fuck?" I roared in response.

206

'I wanted that fucker's head for this shit. I liked this coat, too.' She pulled at the material that was now stained with her blood.

"So you punched me?"

She glared at me. *'There was one more back there that hit me. I was about to get my revenge when you picked me up. Dickhead.'*

I laced my hands behind my head and let out a gusty breath. "Just get in the damn truck."

She flipped me off before climbing in and slamming her door shut. I rolled my eyes and got into the cab. I didn't waste any time cranking the engine and turning on the heat. The cold might not bother me, but that didn't mean I liked it, not to mention, Sirens were similar to humans in their durability.

I pulled out my phone and sent a text to the Priestess to find out where she wanted me to take the fur we'd just collected, then entered the address of the closest safehouse. I needed to check her wound, even if she was pissed at me.

I ignored the ping of my phone as a message came through. I knew it was the Priestess with instructions. I was too worried about the wound in Theia's shoulder. How much pain was she in? Had any splinters remained?

207

I glanced over at her to see her shrugging out of her coat with a pinched look on her face. Next, she pulled her shirt over her head.

"What the hell are you doing?" I asked in shock.

"Road," she snapped in a distorted voice and jabbed her finger at the windshield.

I jerked my head back to the road. "We'll be at the next safehouse in fifteen minutes. I'll check your shoulder there and make sure it's clean. I'm not going to let you heal over debris and shit."

She huffed and pulled her shirt back over her head. We rode in strained silence the rest of the way to the safehouse. The need to check her wound was almost enough to make me pull over right then and there, but I knew there were better supplies under the sink, a standard in all Lycan safehouses.

When we reached the safehouse, she didn't even bother to put her coat back on, despite the light snow falling around us. Her booted feet crunched through the three-inch accumulation up to the door, where she waited with an impatient glare on her face.

"Brat," I muttered, punching in the code and opening the door. She marched inside without a word and headed straight for the bathroom. I shook my head as she started digging through the cabinets.

"The first aid kit is under the sink in all our safehouses. Get your bratty little ass out here and let me see what that furry little bastard did."

She huffed again and made her way to the kitchen. Without a word, I picked her up and sat her on the counter to get a better look at her shoulder. She slapped my hands away, and I let out a huff of frustration. "Quit, brat. I'm removing your shirt to get a better look—just behave for once, would you?"

She rolled her eyes, then pulled her shirt over her head and looked away from me while I examined her wound. Luckily, it looked like there was no debris left behind. I quickly used a saline flush before applying a large bandage over what appeared to be a wound only about an inch-deep.

"There, now you can go back to being a brat and annoying me."

She rolled her eyes and hopped down from the counter, not bothering to pull her shirt back on. I watched as she made her way to the duffel and pulled out clothing before going to the bathroom and closing the door behind her. Irritation radiated off her in waves.

With a sigh, I put away the first aid kit and then pulled out my phone to check the message from the Priestess and find out where we were headed to next. Honestly, the sooner I could get rid of the nasty-smelling Agropelter fur, the better.

There is an Ogre family in Klickitat, Washington. Drop the fur off to them so they can make the wicks and candles. I'll pick them up when they are done.

At least she would pick up the candles herself; that meant I didn't need to do anything more than drop off the fur. I pulled up the GPS on my phone and entered the address she'd sent me to see how long it would take to get there. According to the GPS, it was only going to take a few hours to reach the address.

Leaving my phone on the counter, I went and sat on the couch with my head back and my eyes closed. This entire experience had been exhausting. We'd been traveling for nearly three weeks now. Three weeks of being close to her, touching her, but not having her. Three weeks of craving every part of her.

I opened my eyes and looked in the direction of the bathroom. We could leave as soon as she got out and be there before dark, or we could stay one more night in Oregon and head out in the morning.

My phone pinged, drawing me from my thoughts. As I got up to check it, Theia came out of the bathroom and made her way

210

to the couch in clean clothing, with no evidence of the wound she'd earned from the Agropelter.

'Take a picture; it'll last longer,' she signed before flopping down on the couch and stretching out.

I rolled my eyes, then picked up my phone. When I saw the message was from the Priestess, I braced myself for yet another task. What would it entail this time? Did I have to fight the Ogres? Were they in another dimension, and she forgot to tell me? Or maybe something needed to be done to the Agropelter fur before I could give it to them.

The text that I opened wasn't any of those things. It was simple instructions on how the Ogres would be paid by the Priestess when she picked up the candles.

`Oh, and Lycan, you can't get any more bound to the Siren than you already are. Did I mention a ball gag? It hurts less, but it is still exciting.`

I just stood there, staring at the phone and re-reading the message over and over again. For weeks, I'd made her wear that collar. Weeks during which she'd suffered every time she'd made a sound. And now the Priestess was telling me it was pointless?

My grip tightened around the phone, so tightly that I could hear it starting to crack the protective case. I wanted to throw

211

it—needed to throw it—but it was the only link I had to where we were going. To the Priestess. To whatever came next.

I dropped it on the counter before spinning and kicking a chair so hard that it skittered across the floor and slammed into the kitchen counter where it broke.

Theia sat up with a start and just looked at me without a word.

"Pointless," I growled, my voice shaking. "She says it's *fucking pointless* now?" My chest heaved.

Across the room, Theia sat silently on the couch, her collar still locked in place, watching me as if I were the monster in a cage.

And maybe I was.

Theia...

I just sat there and watched Jackson's outburst. *Pointless?* What the hell was in that text message?

I could hear the *fump-fump* in my ears as my heart rate spiked and my stomach twisted. Had the Priestess told him I was his mate, and this was his reaction? Was the severing spell useless now, and was he furious that he was bound to me for eternity?

He braced himself on the counter, chest heaving as he struggled for control. Then he looked at me, his eyes dark, his brow furrowed, before hanging his head again and letting out a gusty breath.

And then he started toward me.

I lifted my chin and sat still, refusing to flinch. If he'd finally learned the truth that had been in front of him all this time, then so be it.

He crouched in front of me, shaking his head. "This is so fucked up. This whole fucking time, you've been working with me. You've cooked for me and… all kinds of other shit. Damn it."

He dropped his head again, and I couldn't help myself as I reached out and stroked his hair.

He looked up, and his hand came to my cheek, warm fingers cupping it gently. "Do you promise not to run?"

Shock rolled through me. *He's afraid I'll run?* That's what this was about? Not anger… not rage that I might be his mate?

"Do you promise to keep helping me with the list the Priestess sent?"

'Promise,' I signed.

If he still wanted to sever the bond, fine. I could live with that, even as something cracked in my chest.

His hand dropped from my face, and he pressed his thumb to the collar, unlocking it with a soft click.

213

"Try not to entrap anyone else, okay?" he said, the ghost of a smile on his lips.

My hand flew to my throat, fingers grazing the space where the collar had rested for nineteen days. *Was this real? A trick? A dream?*

"The Priestess explained I can't get any more entrapped," he said, his voice hoarse. "She told me the collar was pointless."

Then he rested his head on my knee.

"I thought I had to," he said in a pleading voice that left me stunned.

214

__Chapter 19__

Theia...

Even without the collar, I hadn't spoken to him most of the night. Now, as we drove down the road to deliver fur to some family of Ogres in Washington, I stared out the window. We hadn't spoken when we stopped for lunch either. He'd never once said I was his mate. Did that mean he still thought I'd entrapped him? I had no idea if I wanted to tell him the truth or not.

"I thought you'd talk more, considering you were constantly signing and insulting me and shit," Jackson broke the silence that had been weighing between us as we pulled up to a large farmhouse, snow blown up around the porch in small drifts.

"Guess I'm just used to you barking at me every time I open my mouth, if the last nineteen days are any indication," I said as I sat up and glanced at him.

215

"There it is, that bratty little attitude. I should have known if I tried getting you to talk, it would be this shit," he said in an aggravated tone without even looking at me. He'd hardly looked at me since he took the collar off last night.

"You had a bark collar on me for three weeks and handcuffs! What kind of attitude am I supposed to have? Gods, Jackson, you really are a dense fucking male." Last night, he'd been remorseful about the way he'd treated me, but now he was acting like a fucking dick.

"You entrapped me! You sang your little fucking song and cursed me to crave you like a damn crackhead! Of course, I took precautions! It's what I'm trained to do!"

Before I could respond, an Ogre knocked on the truck window behind Jackson's head, startling us.

"Saved by the Ogre," I muttered. Then I got out of the truck, not wanting to deal with him any longer. Another Ogre stood not far from us. The one closest to us, the one who had knocked on the window, had no glamour or spell hiding his appearance, while the other looked like an older human female in her forties.

"What do you two want?" the female who still held her glamour demanded, shooting a glance at the young male on Jackson's side of the truck.

"A Priestess gave me your address," Jackson said, shooting me a reprimanding glare. "She had us collect some Agropelter hair because she wants you to make candles with it and use the hair for the wicks."

I crossed my arms and held his gaze. "Don't mind him, he's all bark and no bite. Could I use your bathroom? We've been driving for like four hours or more," I finally turned to face the female, effectively dismissing Jackson.

"You're a Siren. Is he under your control?" the female asked, her glamour dropping. I watched as her pale, flushed skin shifted to a grayish-brown tone. Her ears enlarged with drooping lobes, and small tusks protruded slightly from her lower jaw.

I rolled my eyes. "Why does everyone think that's all we do? I don't have time to housebreak a puppy."

She busted out into laughter, while Jackson let out a low growl. "Come inside; there is a bathroom down the hall to relieve yourself." She turned to look at Jackson. "Bring the fur, and we will discuss this inside where it is warmer."

"My name's Kevin. My mom wasn't happy when I came out here, but I could smell you. Don't Lycans hunt Sirens?" the other Ogre asked Jackson in a hushed tone, but not low enough to keep me from hearing.

"Yes," Jackson answered in a tight voice.

217

I climbed up the porch steps, ignoring him. I focused on the crunch of the ice melt under my boots. As I followed the female into the house, I was overwhelmed with the smell of fresh-cut grass, the scent of Ogres. I had to wonder how many of them lived in this house, for the scent to be that strong to me.

"**R**ight down the hall there, on the left," the female said before turning to Jackson and Kevin. "Kevin, take him to have a seat in the kitchen, and see if he wants any tea. I'll wait for the female."

"Theia. My name is Theia," I said before shutting the bathroom door.

"**I**'m Wilma," she said once I came out of the bathroom. It was a little strange to me that she'd not talked through the door or even come in. My sisters would have come in or talked through the door.

"**T**hanks for letting me use the bathroom. I know most immortals hate Sirens." It was a fact that my sisters and I were well aware of.

"**I**'m not most immortals. I'd ask you to not use your powers on my family, but I don't think that's an issue with you." She regarded me with a quizzical look before nodding in the direction Jackson and Kevin had gone.

"Not really, I prefer not to have the burden." I followed her into the kitchen, where Jackson sat with Kevin at a long table that could easily seat a dozen.

"You are full of jokes," she said, as she turned a half-smile toward me. "Do you want any tea or hot chocolate? My daughter insists on the kind with mini marshmallows."

"Sheila said we were out before she went to town with Dad," Kevin supplied, as he sat at the table and braided the fur we'd gathered. To my surprise, he already had a few inches woven together, seamlessly.

"Hot tea will be fine. I appreciate your hospitality," I said, as I took a seat at the table, feeling a little out of place even in the homey atmosphere. I looked around the kitchen, taking it all in. It was well lit and neat as a pin. The countertops wrapped around three walls, and the table held its own space in the open-concept area.

"How did you get the fur? If you don't mind me asking," Wilma asked, as she pulled a mug out of the cabinet for tea.

"We tracked them for three days before catching them. Then another launched a stick into my shoulder, but dickhead over there wouldn't let me get my revenge," I said with a nod at Jackson.

"Really? You're still pissed about that? I got you out of harm's way, you're welcome."

"No one called for Lassi to save Timmy from the well," I said dismissively, pointedly not looking at him.

"No fighting at the table," another Ogre said as she came into the room.

"Grandma, meet Theia and Jackson. They brought some Agropelter fur for us to use as wicks for candles," Kevin said by way of introduction.

"Powerful candles. You lot are mixed up with a spellcaster, then?" the female asked, as she kissed Kevin on the top of his head before sitting between the two of us.

"A Priestess who likes to give random bits of information," Jackson said as he stared daggers at me.

"Hmm, Kevin, how long until that first wick is done?" She turned her attention to her grandson.

"Maybe ten minutes," he said as he continued weaving the fur. "We already discussed payment while Mom was showing Theia to the bathroom."

"That's good." The female turned and looked at me. It was strange seeing a female who looked my age being called grandma. While I was immortal, my sisters and I had spent most

220

of our time around humans. "Why are you traveling with the Lycan if you don't get along?"

"We're working together toward a common goal before we can part ways." I shot a glance at him, hoping we could just part ways, and not part with my life.

The microwave beeped where Wilma had been heating water for my tea the quick way. "She's promised not to go around entrapping males once we finish up this business together," Jackson said, holding my gaze.

The female leaned over and stage-whispered in my ear, "Is he mad you've not had your way with him yet?"

"MOM!" Wilma exclaimed as she set the tea down in front of me, where I laughed.

"Goddess," Jackson muttered and rubbed his face. "When can I tell the Priestess the candles will be ready?"

"Horny old Ogre," Kevin muttered with a look of disgust on his face.

"I can't help it if I miss your grandfather while he's off in another realm visiting his rotten brother," she said with a good-natured smile.

"He's been grumpy since I met him. I think it's just how he is," I said before taking a drink of the tea I'd been given.

221

"To answer your question about the candles, late tonight or even tomorrow, we have the wax already, so it's just a matter of making the candles and letting them harden," Kevin interjected before his grandmother could say anything else.

"How old are you?" I asked him, unable to help myself.

"Eighteen. If I were human, I'd be out on my own by now, but here I am, making candle wicks while my grandma eyeballs a Lycan. Sorry, dude," he said, the last part to Jackson.

"Don't worry about it," Jackson said as he shifted in his seat, still holding his gaze on me.

Wilma tilted her head before sitting down next to her son and picking up some fur. "I suppose the truce between the two of you is tense, based on the way you're watching each other. Once you finish your tea, you can get going, unless you need a place to stay. I suppose we could figure something out."

"I've got a compound not far from here that my pack uses."

She raised her brow and looked up from weaving the fur. "A compound?"

"It's more like an underground bunker. It's from the Cold War."

"I always knew you'd put me in a hole in the ground," I muttered before taking another sip of my tea.

"You're such a brat," Jackson shot back in response.

"Sounds like she needs to be spanked, can I watch?"

"Ew, Grandma, quit," Kevin said as he shot a disgusted look at her while tea came out of my nose.

"I've threatened that before," Jackson added, a dark smile pulling at the corner of his lips.

Heat flooded my lower stomach at the thought, but I still snapped back a smart-ass retort. "Go drag your ass in the snow."

"The two of you are the best entertainment I've had in a while. Why don't you stay for dinner?" the older female invited.

"As long as it isn't frozen food, she'll bitch about it," Jackson answered for us. I was a little surprised by his response.

"I'm an Ogre, not some instant gratification seeking human," Wilma said with a hint of offense in her tone.

"What's your name?" I asked the horny grandma Ogre.

"Livia, I was wondering if you were just going to call me grandma like everyone else around here."

Chapter 20

Theia…

After having an early dinner with the Ogre family, which consisted of Livia, her husband Franko, Wilma, her husband Peter, and their two children, Jackson and I made our way to the compound. The tension between Jackson and me remained. It wasn't like before, when I was determined to make holding me captive a pain in the ass. This was an awkward tension, laced with anger from our earlier argument.

We pulled up to the compound, and I grabbed the duffel, leaving him to grab the cooler. I followed him to the door since I wouldn't be able to open it anyway. He opened it, and I walked by him, dropping the duffel at the bottom of the short flight of steps and just past a second door.

"I forgot my drink in the truck," I muttered, brushing past him on my way back up the steps.

224

"You're not going to tell me to go fetch it for you like a good little dog? No snide comment? I have to wonder, when you fully entrap someone, do they do whatever you say without question?" he demanded as he followed me back out into the snow, just outside the alcove of the entrance.

I stopped and whirled on him, unable to take it any longer. He kept demanding that I'd entrapped him, that this was all my fault, when I'd done nothing! The pain and anger swirling inside me were too much.

"Damn it, Jackson! I never entrapped you! I never so much as hummed a single fucking tune." I glared at him as the snow came down around us. "This"—I waved my hand between us—"isn't my doing. You're not entrapped. You're fucking bonded, at least until the severing spell fixes this shit."

He just stared at me like I'd grown an extra head. "You never sang." It wasn't a question; it was a statement he breathed into the frosted air in a near whisper.

I swallowed convulsively, feeling the weight of his realization settle on him as he looked at me. "Not once."

"I'm not even partially entrapped?"

"Partial entrapment wears off in less than an hour. You would have known before I even regained consciousness that first night."

225

"You're my mate."

My chest was tight, and my throat had gone dry at his admission. He finally realized the truth. What was he going to do now? Was his silence anger that I hadn't told him all this time? Would he have believed me if I'd told him before?

He closed the space between us in an instant, his lips crashing into mine in a brutal kiss. One of his arms wrapped around my waist, pulling me flush against him while the other gripped the back of my neck, his fingers at the base of my skull. The kiss was all-consuming.

He turned me and walked me backward, still kissing me, out of the snow that was coming down heavier now. "It's not a spell," he said against my lips as we bounced into the wall of the alcove relief evident in his tone.

"No," I answered before my teeth nipped at his bottom lip. I was starved for this—for him. Since I'd met him, I'd been starved for him. I'd thought it was just the itch, but my throat was fine. It was my body and mind that wanted him. I loved his dominance, his smell, and his touch.

We stumbled into the compound, Jackson closing the door behind us as he twisted me around, shoving my coat off and pushing me back against the wall at the top of the steps. He shrugged out of his coat and pulled my hips into him, his hand

226

wrapping around my throat. His thumb pressed just over my vocal cords as he nipped at my ear. He picked me up and packed me down the steps before my back was against another wall and my feet were on the floor again.

"Sing your little Siren Song. Free me from this never-ending need to be inside you, to claim you, possess you. Sing and free me from the need to pleasure myself as well as you, because I don't know how long I can hold myself back," he said as he slipped his hand into my pants and stroked between my legs. "Entrap me so I don't have to fight the bond any longer."

"Jackson," I gasped, then put my hands on his chest. "Stop. I don't want this," I said, wanting it, but wanting so much more.

He growled deep in his throat and stepped away from me. "Don't fucking lie to me. I can smell how much you want me to touch you there."

The look of frustration in his eyes, coupled with the tension in his body, should have made me uncomfortable, but instead, it only fueled me. "Stop talking," I said, and pulled my shirt over my head, then leaned down and unlaced my boots.

"Oh hell. You little fucking tease," he growled.

I looked up at him to see him breathing heavily and staring at me with hungry eyes. "Why don't you take off your wet clothes and test how much of a tease I am?"

"You're playing with fire, brat," he said, even as he ripped his shirt over his head. "I want nothing more than to strip us both and bury myself inside you. Is that what you want? For me to admit that you make me ache for you? That I've been going insane wanting you for the last three weeks?"

"No," I said, straightening and unbuttoning my pants. "I want you to undress so I can see what it's like to satisfy those desires." There was no turning back after that one. He held completely still for a split second, and then he was wrapping his arms around me and lifting me off the floor.

"If you change your mind, I don't know if I'll hear you," he said, his breathing heavy as he tossed me on the bed, pushed out of his pants, and reached for my panties. "Fuck, I want to hate you for wanting you this much," he growled as he pulled off my panties and tossed them in the pile of clothes on the floor.

"I'm not stopping you," I said as he settled himself on top of me. A low growl sounded in his throat, and he began kissing me. His hand slipped down and grabbed my leg, lifting me. I could feel the hot tip of his erection pressing against my core. My heart was pounding in my ears.

"Please," I breathed, arching my hips into him. The plea was a loaded one. I wanted him inside me more than I wanted oxygen, but I also wanted it to be more than what I'd experienced all those years ago. I wanted it to be more than him satisfying an urge and not caring if I derived pleasure or pain from the experience.

He held himself just outside of me. "You've no idea what that word does to me," he rasped in my ear. "I want you to beg for it, to want me deep inside you, fucking you like no male has ever fucked you before." His breath tickled against my ear as he pushed just the tip inside and then pulled back, teasing us both.

"Jackson," I rasped in desperation.

"I know you've denied me because I'm a Lycan. Now I want you to know what you've been missing, what you've been denying yourself," he said as he pushed just a little further in and pulled back. "I want every other male you've ever had to look as pathetic as they really are in comparison to me, to what I can do to you."

"Damn it, Jackson! You're already more than he was," I said in exasperation as I wrapped my legs around his hips in an attempt to pull him inside.

He growled and plunged into me, causing me to gasp in pleasure. "If you say another's name, I'll hunt him down and kill him in front of you," he snarled.

"Just you," I gasped as he moved, pleasure like I'd never experienced in my 12,000 years exploding inside me. I laced my fingers in his hair and pulled his face to mine for a kiss. His tongue slipped into my mouth, mocking the thrusting of his body, and I whimpered against his lips. He pulled away from the kiss, began nipping along my jaw, and nipped at my ear.

"Jackson, oh Gods, don't stop," I gasped, keeping rhythm with his movements.

"Not until you cum, again and again," he panted next to my ear.

And just like that, an earth-shattering release ripped through me. The tension tore through my body, the pleasure so intense I began to see spots. I could feel myself clutching at him, gripping him inside and out, as a sound I'd never made escaped from deep in my throat. My body arched up into his, needing him deeper and unable to take any more of him. He wrapped his arms around me and held me tight against him, burying his face in my neck as he pumped his hips and snarled before giving one last shuddering thrust into me.

He held me like that, both of us breathing in ragged, shuddering breaths.

"I'm going to do that again and again, until you can't remember any other male."

"I'm good with that," I said, my heart pounding in my ears. "Just let me," panting in between words, "remember how to breathe first."

He nipped at my neck. "Did you have to ask that of any of the others? Did they make you orgasm so hard you had to fight to breathe?"

"Jackson," I said in a soft voice, closing my eyes. "I've only ever had sex with one other male, and he never satisfied anyone but himself. Now stop ruining this for me."

"One?" he asked in disbelief.

"Bad dog, drop it," I said, knowing it would rub him the wrong way but not wanting him to put two and two together about my lost son.

He lifted himself and looked down at me. I braced myself for the backlash of his anger after calling him a dog.

"You've not had sex in 12,000 years?"

"Seriously? Get off me," I snapped, shoving against his chest.

231

He grabbed my hands and held me still. "You told me you had a son before you became immortal, and if you've only ever had sex with one other male, then you are referring to the father of your child. Your barb at my canine attributes will not distract me from the facts. Was he human?"

I glared up at him, hating that I was struggling to keep from crying. "He was my first kill," I said in a cold tone.

"Good," he said, then leaned forward and kissed me gently. I felt the tension melt from my body, his grip on my hands releasing as he cupped my face. He broke the kiss. "I still intend to erase his touch from your mind, in every position possible," he said, then rolled me over onto my stomach. "Lift yourself for me," he said in a tight voice.

I felt oddly embarrassed. Then again, I'd never willingly been in this position before, but I did as he said. He gripped my hips, and I felt him press into me as he leaned forward and kissed my back. "You're mine, Theia."

I gasped as Jackson began thrusting into me, the pleasure immediate and overwhelming. He wrapped one arm around my waist, kneading my breast with rough, possessive hands, while the other braced against the mattress. I could barely hold myself up as he slammed deep inside me, his balls slapping against my clit with every thrust. It was brutal—so deep, so relentless—that it

232

straddled the line between pleasure and pain. But Gods, it only made everything sharper, rawer.

The way he moved, primal, hungry, like he was claiming what had always been his, broke something open in me. "I'll never let you go," he rasped next to my ear as he pressed me into the mattress. And then he bit down, sinking his fangs into the curve of my neck. I cried out in surrender as another orgasm ripped through my body.

Jackson shook above me, his breathing ragged as he kissed the bite he'd just left.

"My mate. You're mine. My brat. My little pain in the ass."

I could feel the smile on his lips buried in the curve of my neck.

"I'd say, 'Bad dog, no biting,' but I kinda liked it," I said with a smile of my own.

"Brat," he said as he bit me again, lighter this time and on the edge of the shoulder. He shifted so that his weight was no longer pinning me down and slapped my ass playfully.

"Let's go take a shower, and maybe when we're done, we can get cleaned up."

I laughed and shook my head. "You're terrible."

He got out of bed and chuckled, low and sexy.

233

"I told you before, if it was your pussy I was fucking, you wouldn't be able to walk."

He grabbed my hand and tugged gently.

"Now come join me in the shower, because I'm nowhere near done with you."

Chapter 21

Theia...

I woke warm and happy, if a little annoyed by my bladder. Jackson lay behind me, sleeping soundly. After the things he'd done to me, I wasn't surprised, even with my immortal healing, my muscles felt the strain of what we'd done only hours ago.

I scooted out of the bed and tiptoed to the bathroom, not wanting to wake him. After relieving my bladder, I walked over to the sink, began to wash my hands, and looked down—as I always did—at my palm, at my son. And my heart stopped.

Panic set in as I turned up both hands to find them empty. There was no seahorse, my son was gone. Shutting off the water, I snatched the towel off the wall and dried my hands, looking over my legs. They were unmarked. I dropped the towel on the floor and began twisting my body around, inspecting every inch of skin

235

I could, even going as far as lifting my hair to check the back of my neck in the mirror.

My chest grew tight, my breathing panicked as I clutched at my throat. I couldn't breathe. *He was gone.* What had happened to my baby? Why was he *gone*? My heart was pounding in my ears, roaring so loudly I wasn't sure if I could hear anything at all.

Closing my eyes, I forced myself to take a deep breath. Poseidon would know.

I looked at the closed door. He would never let me go, not after last night. Taking a steadying breath, I opened the door. Jackson was still asleep in the bed. I tiptoed over and began picking up my clothes from yesterday. I pulled everything on, keeping my eyes on the sleeping Lycan, then picked up my boots. I decided it would be better to put the boots on at the door so I wouldn't make as much noise walking.

Glancing at the duffle that lay open from our shower last night, I decided to grab the shock collar. If Poseidon gave me back my son, then I would use the collar to find my way back to Jackson. I would put the collar on, hang a sign around my neck that read *"Property of the Lycan Jackson,"* and march myself across the country.

If Poseidon didn't give back my son, then I would end it. I couldn't bear the thought of an eternity without him. Instead, I would gladly feed myself to sharks, gators, or a pack of hungry wolves.

Setting the boots down at the door, I slipped my feet into them and laced them up as quickly as I could.

Closing my eyes, I took another calming breath through my nose and wrapped my fingers around the door handle.

I looked back at Jackson through the open bedroom door, then opened the one in front of me as quietly as I could.

No movement.

I decided that letting the door latch behind me was too risky, since I still had a flight of steps and another door between me and my best chance of escape. I pulled it nearly shut, thanking the heavens it wasn't squeaky, and hurried up the steps as silently as I could, grabbing my discarded jacket along the way and pulling it on.

At the top of the steps, I shook out my arms to ready myself, then opened the door and closed it behind me as I bolted into the trees.

It wasn't long before I heard the echo of my name behind me in a roar of grief and anger. Jackson had woken up.

My heart pounded in my ears as I ran, nearly loud enough to drown out the sound of my breathing as I moved through the night, my feet pounding through the ankle-deep snow.

I had no idea what time it was, or even where I was going, but I had to get to the ocean as quickly as possible.

I had to get Theo back, and then I could return to Jackson.

I could hear his howl in the distance as he shifted. He was getting closer with each second that passed. Would I be able to outrun him long enough to get away? Should I have put the collar on him instead? Should I have broken his neck? Could I have broken his neck?

Suddenly, the trees were gone, and I nearly face-planted on the pavement as I reached a road. Headlights glared in my eyes, and I lifted my arms to shield my face as I heard the squeal of brakes. I'd braced myself for impact—the wrong impact. Jackson tackled me, twisting his body as we flew through the air, landing in the snowdrift on the other side of the road. He lifted himself over me and snarled.

"Theia!" I heard Ella's voice call out.

As the snarling wolf on top of me twisted to look at my sister, I kicked his chest, knocking him off me, and shoved to my feet.

"Run!" I yelled, not sure who I was shouting the warning to.

Before I could get to my sister, a Grizzly shifter leaped into my path from the trees, charging at me.

I twisted around to run from him, only to have Jackson leap at me.

I ducked and rolled out of the way, the only thing I could do with an attacker on either side of me.

The sound of the Grizzly in pain made me pause as I got to my feet.

Jackson was attacking the Grizzly, an angry whirl of teeth and claws as they slashed at each other, red tinting the snow.

"Theia! Get in the truck!" Ella yelled at me. I noticed a Vampire getting out, a gun aimed at them.

Jackson's yelp of pain pulled my attention back to them. The Grizzly threw him into a tree, and I watched, horrified, as Jackson didn't move.

"NO!" I roared and charged the shifter, my feet slipping in the slush of the road as I changed direction.

The Grizzly hit all fours and came at me full speed as I quickly gained my momentum.

Ella's screaming was an odd static sound in my ears as I charged the massive shifter.

I dropped at the last second, reaching up and grabbing the Grizzly by his jaws, sliding under him.

He twisted, his massive body flipping from the momentum of the move.

As he landed, I twisted my body up, landing my feet on his massive shoulders.

My grip tightened, and I fell into a squat, bracing myself.

I began to twist as I pulled up, pushing off with my legs, all in such a short span of time that the Grizzly was only able to scratch an ankle before his head ripped from his body.

The sickening crunching sound that came from his neck was the most satisfying sound I'd ever heard.

I fell backward, the shifter's head in my hands, blood and spinal fluid soaking me.

"Shit," came Ella's stunned reaction.

"Bloody hell," said the Vampire at the same time, with a slight British accent.

I laid my head back in the slush on the road and closed my eyes, breathing heavily as I fought to catch my breath.

"Theia, come on, let's go," Ella said from above me, and I opened my eyes to see her extending a hand.

"I'll take care of the Lycan," said the Vampire.

"Don't fucking touch him," I snarled, shoving to my feet, still holding the head. Ella backed away from me as I walked over to Jackson. I tossed the head at him, then fell into a squat and checked his pulse. The blow had knocked him unconscious. Part of me was glad; the other part of me had hoped he would have been temporarily killed, giving us more of a head start. I shoved to my feet. "We need to go, now," I said as I walked toward the truck that was half up on a snowdrift on the far side of the road.

"You just ripped the head off a Grizzly with your bare hands; we have time for one of us to do the same to the Lycan," Ella said, turning toward Jackson.

I grabbed her and punched her in the face so hard that she staggered back. "I said, don't *fucking* touch him!"

She looked stunned, a look I'd never seen on my sister's impassive face before. "Did you really just hit me?"

"We need to get to the ocean as soon as possible. Don't make me waste time kicking your ass," I said in a shaky voice.

"The ocean," she repeated, looking mildly confused, her shocked expression gone.

I held out my palm. "Tell me you found Kassie, because I need both of you to help me call Poseidon," my voice shook with an edge of desperation.

"Fin, let's go, now," she said, turning and marching with me toward the truck.

"What about the Lycan?" he asked, looking completely lost.

"Someone needs to clean up the Grizzly shifter; let him do it," I said.

241

"He's not just going to forget about you and let you go just because you gave him a severed head," the vampire, Fin, said as I climbed into the truck.

Ella pulled the shock collar out of my back pocket. "What's this?" she asked.

"Give it back," I said, snatching it from her.

"Is that a bark collar?" Fin asked.

"A what?" Ella asked.

"Ocean! Now," I snapped, not wanting to waste any time. I was barely keeping it together.

"We can talk on the way to the safehouse to get Kassie and Clay," Ella said as she climbed into the truck.

"Clay? As in Sasquatch?" I asked, my turn to be shocked that he was still alive.

"Kassie is his mate," Ella said, as if that explained why she hadn't killed him. "Now, spill about the collar."

"It's a shock collar; once it's on your neck, it shocks you if you say anything, keeping a Siren from using her powers," I said, not wanting to talk about it. I knew I was suffering from a serious case of Stockholm Syndrome, but I didn't give a damn at the moment as I thought of how I'd just had mind-blowing sex with the male who had put the thing on me.

242

Ella and Fin exchanged a look. Then Ella asked, "So what are you planning on doing with it?"

"Shutting you up," I snapped.

"I'm going to let that slide." She twisted around and looked at me, then her eyes narrowed. "What is that on your neck? Are you injured?"

I pulled my jacket up to cover Jackson's bite and glared at her. "I'm fine."

She rolled her eyes before unbuckling and climbing to the back with me.

"What the hell! Ella!" Fin exclaimed, the truck he'd just gotten back on the road was swerving.

"Keep it on the road, leech. Theia, let me see your wound." Ella pulled out her phone and turned on the light.

"It's fine, you nut job," I insisted as I held my hand over the mark.

"What if there is something in it? How bad is the bleeding? Do you want to lose consciousness before we get back to Clay and Kassie?"

"It's almost healed," I said as I tried pushing her hands away again.

"It looks like a bite mark," Fin said from the front seat.

"Did that dog bite you?" Ella demanded.

243

"Yes, now can we please just get to the ocean as fast as possible?" I asked as tears began to spill from my eyes. I needed to know what had happened to Theo. Why had my son disappeared from my hand?

"Fin will get us there," she said in a softer tone.

As we drove, I began to shiver, my wet clothing finally registering. When I'd slid under the bear, snow and slush had gone up my shirt as well as soaking through my pants. I was a mess.

I looked down at myself, but was unable to see through my own tears that refused to stop. Theo was *gone*, and I'd run from Jackson after he'd made me promise not to. I'd decided to live, and my son was taken from me. How was I supposed to keep going without him?

A sob ripped out of my throat as I looked at my empty palm.

Ella wrapped her arms around me, and I buried my face in her shoulder as she held me. My sister, who seemed to be made of stone, was trying to comfort me, and all I felt was earth-shattering, soul-wrenching pain.

Chapter 22

Theia...

Ella had told me how Fin was *her* male as we'd drove. The shock that should have come over me with her confession was little more than an echo in the swirling void of sorrow that engulfed me.

When we'd reached the safehouse, Ella had sent Fin in to get Kassie and Clay. We were back on the road within ten minutes, Ella and Kassie on either side of me in the back seat, and Clay following behind us in our truck. Fin had managed to get us to what he said was a company-owned safehouse just before dawn, with a private beach.

The sky was just beginning to lighten as the Vampire ducked inside the safehouse with a duffel bag. I looked at the ocean, then the beach house. Through the open door, I watched as Ella put her hands on either side of Fin's head, pulling him in for a kiss. Then, in a swift motion, she snapped his neck, and his body dropped.

"Clay, shift and make sure no sun hits him. We need to sing," Ella's voice held an edge as she stepped back from the body of her male.

Her action tickled the surface of the well of pain I was in for only a moment before I turned and walked toward the ocean. Each step squelched and tugged as the wet sand clung to the soles of my booted feet. The closer I grew to the waterline, the heavier each step became, the weight of the silence in this place broken only by the sound of the waves on the shore in the cold morning air. A mist began to rise just as I reached the water's edge.

"Poseidon, I need you," I whispered as the waves crashed against the shore in the dense fog. I looked at my palm, where for twelve thousand years the seahorse had rested, representing my lost son, his soul forever tied to my immortal body. The smooth, unmarked skin hurt more than any wound I'd sustained in my entire existence.

Kassie and Ella approached then, each holding out a hand silently to either side of me.

"The last time we called him, we all sang together," Kassie said softly.

I remembered how we'd brought down Atlantis, with all the men in the city under our thrall, how Poseidon had appeared and given Theo back in that unexpected way.

"I broke Fin's neck, and apparently, Clay is immune as long as he's in his animal form. We have nothing to worry about," Ella elaborated, still holding her hand out to me.

My own hands shook as I laced my fingers through theirs. I looked between the two of them before inhaling and beginning to vocalize. None of us used words, our vocalizations blending together as we stood on the shore and let loose our siren's call.

***

Theia...

I don't know how long we'd sung before we stopped. Now it was just a waiting game. Kassie and Ella had gone back inside after I told them I needed to be alone. Now I sat on the shore with a blanket wrapped around my shoulders that Kassie had brought out. Each of them had tried to join me, only for me to tell them again to leave me.

I'd raged and screamed at them. I'd sobbed and choked on my own snot and sorrow. I'd pushed them away with words, gasped between gut-wrenching sobs of pain from the repetitive shattering of my heart as Poseidon continued not to show up.

Even as that storm had passed, I'd denied their company on the soggy shore where I stared at the waves.

I couldn't stand it; couldn't stand the pain of them being so close, reminding me of what I still had. I didn't want them, didn't want that anchor to life any longer. If Poseidon didn't give Theo back, I didn't want them to stop me. They each had a male now to lean on. They were healing while my own pain was eating me alive.

I was soaked through from the constant mist that had endured throughout the day, the weight and chill of it all fitting with how I was drawing in my own sorrow. Each tiny *pip-pip* on my skin was another agonizing reminder of my continued life without him, without Theo. I could feel the desperation tightening in my chest.

Pip-pip-pip.

I was done. There was nothing left. Standing, I dropped the blanket Kassie had draped around me and charged into the ocean.

"Poseidon! Where are you?" I cried as the waves pushed and pulled against me, trying and failing to knock me off my feet.

I plunged deeper and deeper into the water until it was up to my waist, the sound of my sisters screaming for me in the background a dull sort of drone, like that of a plane flying overhead.

Another wave crashed as I pushed forward, and a howl filled my ears.

I went down, my head slipping beneath the waves as the ocean pulled me under.

This was it. The icy bite of the water would be my end. My body would be pulled out to sea by the waves, and I'd either drown for eternity, suffering, just as I should for letting Theo slip away, or I'd be eaten by sharks.

I was letting go. Letting myself succumb to the pain of loss.

The water parted away from me, and my body collapsed on the sandy ocean floor. I coughed and sputtered out the freezing water that had filled my lungs as warm arms pulled me into a chest that smelled of tonka and exotic wood.

"Give her a moment to catch her breath," a familiar voice said through the roaring in my ears.

I blinked frantically, wiping the stinging salt water from my eyes. It had been over twelve thousand years, but I knew that voice.

As my vision cleared, I looked at Jackson's face. "He's gone," I gasped, holding up my hand.

249

"Calm yourself, Ameltheia," Poseidon's voice soothed.

I turned my attention to him and ripped myself from Jackson's arms, launching toward his ankles, too weak to stand as the tears flowed down my face.

"Where is my child? Where is Theo?" I sobbed at Poseidon's feet.

"He never left you. Your lost child has simply been waiting for a vessel for his return," Poseidon said, placing his hand on my cheek, causing me to look up at him as the waves brushed around us in a strange circle.

"What do you mean?" I asked in a trembling voice.

"Are you saying my pup has been replaced with another soul?" Jackson asked from behind me.

"Not entirely. It took some doing, but I was able to split the egg. The babies will be your DNA, one a new soul, the other, Theia's lost child," Poseidon said as he looked over my head.

His *pup*—split the egg—*babies*?

I looked at Jackson, who crouched down next to me. "I... I'm pregnant?" I stammered out the question, not sure I'd understood Poseidon correctly.

"We," Jackson growled, narrowing his eyes. "You're not leaving my side ever again, is that understood?"

250

I fell forward into his chest and clung to his naked body, sobbing.

"I'm so sorry, Jackson. I panicked, I didn't think you would understand."

"Poseidon, you will ensure my female does not lose either of her children."

I glanced up at Poseidon to see a smile quirk at the corner of his mouth.

"It has been a very long time since I've encountered anyone bold enough to attempt to give me orders, and it's only made more amusing that you are naked. Take my grandchild inside so that she may recover her senses."

He tilted his head as though he were listening to the waves.

"There are things that have happened while I've been sleeping. Persephone needs to speak with me as well. Strange. I wonder what my sister-in-law needs to speak with me about. Be well, granddaughter."

Before any of us could say another word, Poseidon turned into water and disappeared into the surf.

Jackson lifted me into his arms and carried me to the shore, the water seeming to morph around us and out of the way

251

as I shivered in his arms. My sisters and Sasquatch stood on the shore with a myriad of expressions among them.

"If you intend to harm my female, know that I will gladly end all of you," Jackson said in a deadly calm voice.

"They're my sisters—and Clay," I said in a weak voice.

"And the little dot between your eyes is courtesy of Fin. He's in the house with a sniper rifle loaded with vervain tranquilizer darts. Now relinquish my sister, mutt," Ella said in a calm voice.

"Over my dead body," Jackson snarled.

I put my hand on his chest and leaned my head against him. "Ella, I'm pregnant with his babies. One of them is Theo." I tilted my head to look at my sister. "Poseidon gave him back to me. Jackson won't hurt me."

"She needs to get inside and changed, now." Jackson's voice left no room for argument.

"And you need clothing on," Kassie said as she glanced around and snatched up the blanket I'd cast off. "Here. Gods, this is weird."

Clay snatched it from her and wrapped it around Jackson and me, probably covering next to nothing, but I couldn't see, nor did I care.

252

"I'm sorry," I whispered as Jackson followed my sisters and Clay across the beach.

He didn't look at me. Instead, his eyes scanned each of my sisters and Clay, who had yet to change out of his Sasquatch form. "You should have told me," he said so softly I almost didn't hear him.

Fin stood in the doorway with the gun lowered as he watched us, the sun casting just enough of a shadow over the front of the house to keep him from burning.

"I panicked," I whispered back, knowing he could hear me.

"I know." He looked down at me then. "I've never seen you afraid. I tracked the scent of your fear. Don't let that happen again."

"Lycan, take my sister into the bathroom, and I'll get you both some clothes. Clay should have something that fits you," Kassie said as we entered the house.

"Is anyone going to fill me in? I might have excellent hearing, but you were too far away for me to catch it all." Fin propped the gun next to the door, still regarding Jackson with a cautious look.

"My mate needed to have a talk with her grandfather. Now step back, Vampire," Jackson said as he glared at Fin.

"Theia, your male needs to be housebroken," Ella said, stepping up next to her Vampire.

"Lycan, my name is Fin. This little Songbird is Ella, my bonded female, and she hates males. Talk to her at your own risk. Your mate is shivering." Fin glanced to the left. "Why don't you allow her to get warmed up, and we can all talk like civilized monsters?"

"My name is Jackson. I don't trust any of you."

"The feeling is mutual, I assure you. But my sister needs to get out of those wet clothes, especially being pregnant," Kassie's voice sounded from the left.

"Pregnant?" Fin echoed, glancing at Ella.

"Apparently, she's having puppies. Dog, take my sister to the shower and put some clothes on yourself," Ella demanded, her tone tight.

"Fuck off," I snapped at her, even as Jackson turned and made his way to the bathroom, where Kassie stood with her arms full of clothing for both of us.

"Here, go in that room there and get dressed while I help her out of those wet clothes," Kassie said as she set the clothing in two piles on the counter.

I could feel the tension in his body as he held me. "I'm not leaving her."

254

She rolled her eyes. "Theia, do you want me to remove the dog or not?"

"He's fine," I said, even as Jackson growled. "They don't trust you yet. Now put me down."

Kassie rolled her eyes again and left the room, closing the door behind her. Jackson set me on my feet gently before walking to the shower and turning on the water.

"Lift your arms, brat." The teasing tone he normally had was gone.

This was a soft command, and I did as I was told. He pulled my soaked shirt over my head before turning me around and undoing the hooks of my bra. Next, he knelt in front of me and removed my boots and socks. Sand and water covered his hands and thighs as he cast them aside, then reached up and began pulling my wet pants down, the cold and damp material sticking to my skin.

Once he had stripped me, he gently guided me into the shower. To my surprise, he didn't join me. I stood under the warm spray, letting it warm my shivering body as I listened to him move around the bathroom. Then the curtain moved, and he was in the shower with me. I wiped the water from my eyes and looked up at him.

"Let me wash your hair for you," he said softly as he urged me to turn around. I didn't argue or fight. There was no rebellion or sass left in me. He began to work shampoo into my hair, his fingers massaging my scalp, slow and deliberate.

"Rinse," he commanded, pulling me back to step under the spray again. He worked the lather out of my hair, the suds sliding down my body. He repeated the process with conditioner, his fingers kneading down my neck this time.

My hair now clean, I watched as he worked soap into a lather on the rag he held. He stepped up to me, looking down into my face with his molten amber eyes.

"Don't ever run from me again."

"Never again," I promised as a fresh tear slipped down my face at the guilt I felt.

He pressed a kiss to my forehead as he ran the rag down my arm.

"Good girl. Now let me finish washing you."

The relief in his voice was something I'd never expected.

Chapter 23

Jackson…

I'd washed Theia and helped her get dressed again. Together, we'd left the bathroom and made our way to the couch, where her blonde sister had set two steaming mugs on the coffee table with what smelled like hot chocolate. I handed her a cup after she sat down, then took a seat next to her.

Another male walked out and draped a blanket over the arm of the couch. "Kassie and I are going to make dinner. If you need anything, just let us know. And Lycan, I would advise against talking to Ella unless you want her to break your nose too."

Theia blinked up at him. "I'm sorry I missed that. I'm still mad at you."

He rubbed the back of his neck. "I deserve that. My kind doesn't share much, though. This is new to me."

257

"Go help my sister, Clay." Theia pulled her feet up on the couch and looked away from him.

I watched their interaction, my mind still reeling. My female was *pregnant*. That proved that she was mine. A Lycan couldn't have children with anyone but their mate. All this time, I'd been looking for a way to sever the bond between us, and the Moon Goddess had been the one to create it, not her magic. Not once had she or her sisters tried to entrap me since I'd arrived, even when they didn't trust me. The males who were with her sisters didn't appear to be mindless monsters, but rather males devoted to their mates. Were we wrong about Sirens?

I pulled the blanket from the edge of the couch that Clay had left and wrapped it around Theia. "Here, brat."

"You know, if you change your mind, I'm happy to murder him for you," Ella said as she sat next to Theia a few moments later. I narrowed my eyes at her, not trusting them despite everything I'd learned today.

"Ella, just go away. I'm not in the mood," Theia said without moving from my side, where she was currently nestled, wrapped up in the blanket with her hot chocolate forgotten.

"All I'm saying is, if it ends up turning out you don't want to keep your pet, I'll put the dog down."

I growled at her and tightened my arm around my mate. "I don't think I like your sister."

"In her defense, you did take me and keep me as your prisoner. She's just trying to be a good sister in her own weird way," she looked up at me. "I'm still waiting to wake up. Jackson, I—" She fell silent, her eyes closed, and she laid her head back on my shoulder.

"What is it? You need to talk to me this time before you just run away and cause my Wolf to go insane." The pain in her voice and the lack of fight she normally had made my chest clench in fear. How did I help her? Where was my little brat that drove me crazy with that never-ending snark?

"Fuck," Ella said as she tipped her beer back and turned to leave the room.

"About damn time," I muttered, glad she was leaving.

"Get bent, mutt. I'm giving my sister the space to tell you she loves you. If you don't say it back, I'm going to make you regret it."

"Ella," Theia said as she sat up and threw a couch pillow at her.

"I'll let you get away with that because you're pregnant. Remember, mutt, reciprocate, or pay the price."

259

I put my finger under Theia's chin and tilted her face up to look at me. I needed to see her eyes. There it was, what her sister had said. I needed to hear it, though. "Say it, brat. Tell me how you feel."

Her pupils dilated, and I could smell her desire mingled with fear, that scent I hated to smell on her. "I love you, Jackson."

"Fuck," I said, just before I claimed her mouth. Her hands fisted in my shirt, and I pulled her onto my lap so she was straddling me. "I love you, too."

She gave a shaky laugh and rested her head on my chest, her arms curled between us. I wrapped my arms around her, stroking her back. We sat like that in silence for a few minutes, just holding each other.

"I wasn't running from you. You need to know that," her soft voice broke the silence between us.

"It's okay. I've got you now."

"I'll never run again," she said as she kissed my neck.

"Maybe I should punish you for being a naughty little brat," I said in a harsh whisper as my eyes closed and I tilted my head back, exposing more of my throat to her.

"I'm being serious, Jackson."

"So am I," I said as I grabbed her hips and ground her against the erection I'd had since those three little words left her lips. I pressed my cheek to hers, my lips next to her ear. "Last night I fucked you. Tonight, I wanna make love to you. Then maybe later I'll make you beg for it, when you're feeling a little better."

"Might I suggest somewhere other than the couch for your extracurricular activities?" Fin's voice shocked me. I'd not heard him approach and had been so caught up in the scent of my female, I'd not realized his had grown stronger as he entered the room. "I was sent to tell you that dinner will be ready in about forty-five minutes."

"Thanks," I said, not looking at him. I was torn between the desire to rip him apart for interrupting and feeling like a kid caught with their hand in the cookie jar.

"Jackson," Theia said, drawing my attention. "Please." Her voice dropped to a husky whisper in my ear.

"Vampire, which bedroom is ours?" I asked as I pushed to my feet, Theia wrapping her legs around me.

"End of the hall," he said as he sat down and rubbed the bridge of his nose.

Theia...

Jackson didn't waste a second packing me down the hall to the room Fin had directed us to. He kicked the door shut, then pressed my back to it, his lips locked on mine. My hands were on either side of his head, holding his face to mine. I pulled my hands away from his face and reached between us, pulling at the button on his pants.

He turned and stumbled toward the bed, where he laid me down instead of tossing me. He pulled his shirt over his head and dropped it on the floor. My eyes followed the tribal tattoos going down his chest and up his neck and arms. I sat up and made a move toward him, but he smiled and took a step back.

"Strip." He crossed his arms and held my gaze, that single command hanging in the air between us.

My fingers gripped the hem of my shirt and pulled it over my head, exposing my breasts as I had no bra on. I wiggled out of my pants, kicking them off the bed. Before I could remove my panties, his fingers were gripping my ankles and dragging me to the edge of the bed. His kiss traced a trail down my abdomen to the waistband of my panties before he tugged them out with his teeth and let the elastic snap back against my skin.

He pulled them down, his hot fingers brushing against my hips. "I'm going to have you in every way possible," he said as he kissed my thigh. "Mind, body, and soul."

"I'm yours," I said as my hands came up and I began to knead my breasts. I wanted his mouth on me, wanted his head between my legs, and his teeth on my clit.

"Such a naughty little brat, starting without me," he said as he stepped away from me. He pushed out of his pants, standing naked in front of me. He tugged on his balls before wrapping his hand around his erection. "Be a good girl. Spread those legs for me and let me have a taste before I give it to you."

Gods help me, I was so fucking wet for him. I spread my legs and pulled myself all the way to the edge of the bed before he knelt. "Good girl," he growled before his tongue licked up my center. "Knead those breasts for me. I want you to pinch them until you almost can't stand it," he commanded with another lick.

"Jackson," I breathed, doing as he said.

"Such a good girl."

His hands gripped my ass cheeks almost painfully, and he buried his tongue in my core before his teeth raked over my clit. He sucked hard as they rasped over me, then flicked with his tongue again. He tormented me with his mouth, nipping, sucking, and licking, until I was on the verge of release.

"Not yet, brat," he said as my legs began to tense. He stood. "Roll over. Let me see that gorgeous ass."

263

Heat flushed through my body, but I rolled over, putting myself on my hands and knees at the edge of the bed. "Goddess, you're so fucking sexy." He stroked my ass before slapping my cheek.

"Oh!" I didn't expect it.

"I told you, you need to be punished. You don't get to cum until you beg for me to be buried deep inside you." He ran his hand in a soothing circle over the cheek he'd just slapped. With his other hand, he rubbed the tip of his erection against my swollen and aching center. "You feel that? I know you want it. I know you want me to fuck your brains out, don't you?"

"Yes," I gasped, rocking back.

Smack.

"Not until you say what I want to hear." His hand gripped my hip, and he slipped two fingers inside me, playing with me.

"Please," I panted.

"I like that too, but that's not what I want to hear."

I rocked my hips back, needing his fingers to move faster, needing more. Then his teeth nipped my ass cheek. "Tell me what I want to hear, little mate."

What did he want? "Fuck me, please."

"Such a demanding little brat." His fingers curled, hitting a spot inside that sent a jolt of pleasure through me. "Do I need to

264

spell it out for you? Those three little words I want you to say again?"

"I love you," I said as realization dawned.

"Good girl," he growled as he pulled his fingers from my pussy and replaced them with his cock. He pushed deep inside me, his hands locked on my hips in a bruising grip, and I moaned in satisfaction.

"Say it again," he demanded as he pulled back.

"Make me," I taunted, finally catching on to his game.

He chuckled and thrust forward, hard. "I'll make you all right. I'll nail you to this damn mattress if I have to, but you'll say it at least three more times before I let you cum."

"You're all bark and no bite," I said, my hands fisting in the sheets as he pulled out slowly and deliberately.

Smack.

The sting bloomed over my ass before he rubbed circles again. "You keep talking, brat, but those aren't the words I want."

"Fuck me harder and maybe you'll get what you want," I taunted, loving the hot sting on my ass.

He pulled back and thrust in hard enough that it blurred the line between pleasure and pain. He did it again, pulling out slowly before slamming deep inside.

"Faster," I whimpered, needing more—so much more.

"Say it," he demanded.

"I love you."

"Two more to go," he said before he pulled back and drove forward. His rhythm picked up, faster and faster. "Again," he demanded, spanking me between thrusts.

"I love you," I whimpered, my arms giving out and my fists clenching uselessly in the sheets.

"Fuck, Theia, say it again." He drove himself into me from behind, fast and hard.

"I love you, Jackson, I love you."

His hand fisted in my hair. "You're *mine*, brat. I love you."

I moaned, and my body shuddered as his words washed over me. I was his. He owned me. I'd let him own me. I was his in every way. I belonged to this male.

"Theia," he groaned as I came, my core clenching around him. He took one last shuddering thrust before holding my hips to his, his hot cum filling me.

I cried out his name, a tear slipping down my face from the force of the orgasm he'd just given me. My body quaked, my muscles giving out, and I fell forward, spent.

266

Chapter 24

Theia...

We walked into the kitchen for dinner to find that Kassie and Clay had made spaghetti, meatballs, and garlic bread. It smelled amazing. I picked up a plate, intending to help myself, only to have Jackson pluck it from my hands.

"Sit, brat. I'll get it."

"Fuck you, give me my plate back." I wasn't even sure why I was arguing with him.

"If you're not too sore from what we just did, I guess I'll have to try again after dinner."

"Ew, not at the table, guys," Kassie said as she turned bright red.

"I enjoyed the table," Clay muttered.

"Clay!" Kassie's eyes were impossibly wide as she scolded him, making me snort out an unladylike laugh.

267

"Leech, I've got an idea to run by you later," Ella said as she drummed her fingers on the edge of the table and looked at Fin with a slight curve to her lips.

"Okay, you can get my food for me. I need to sit down after that one." I relinquished my plate to Jackson and sat down, just staring at Ella. I knew she'd said she was keeping Fin, but it hadn't really registered until just now. Seeing my sister address a male directly and suggest they have sex, let alone sex on the kitchen table, was mind-boggling.

"Maybe not this table, Songbird." Fin cast a quick glance at Ella before piling spaghetti on top of a slice of garlic bread and taking a bite.

"I'm thinking eventually we'll get used to it," Kassie said with a stunned look on her face.

"If the two of you are allowed to keep them, I'm allowed to keep mine," Ella said dismissively.

Jackson set a plate in front of me before taking a seat next to me with his own plate. "Clay, why didn't you have a smell in your Sasquatch form?"

"When we shift, we smell like our surroundings," Clay answered in a stiff voice.

"I suppose that's why it isn't common knowledge that you are shifters. My pack was always taught that you were, but

268

instructed not to spread that knowledge. I thought you'd look Indigenous, but you're white," Jackson stated before taking a bite.

"My grandmother was a settler, and so was my father." I watched as Clay seemed to relax as he took his seat, with Kassie between him and Ella. "I didn't realize anyone knew about us at all."

"My pack teaches that long ago, two brothers were picked by the Moon Goddess and blessed with the powers to shift, one into a Wolf, the other a Sasquatch. They were meant to help keep the balance and protect nature. My pack believes they are direct descendants of one of the brothers."

"We have a similar story, but we were not told one of the brothers was a Wolf, only that they were gifted the ability to shift and protect the land," Clay elaborated.

"So you didn't tell us, or even Kassie, that you were Bigfoot the whole time you were taking us deep into the swamp because no one is supposed to know about you?" I pinned Clay with a hard look. My sister had nearly died, a death she would not have come back from, because of him.

"I wasn't sure how to tell any of you. If I had, what would you have done? Had I told you, would you have let me get to know Kassie? I never expected her to show up at the docks to contract a boat, but when she did, I decided to see where things went without her knowing she was my mate."

"You nearly got her killed," I hissed.

"As opposed to kidnapping me and dragging me across the country as his hostage with no word to my sisters after ripping out my vocal cords?" Kassie shot back, not allowing Clay to respond.

"That wasn't me. One of my uncle's pack members took out her vocal cords," Jackson cut in, his body radiating rage.

"They are all dead, by the way. The Lycans you attacked with," Ella added in her bland voice, and the table fell silent.

"You killed them?" Jackson accused in a low voice filled with disbelief and rage.

"No, the Grunch beat me to it. If I'd known this was where things would lead, I would have saved that last one's head for you the way I did for Kassie."

Ella continued to eat as if what she said was completely normal while Jackson stared at her in disbelief. I put my hand on his leg in an effort to comfort him. Had my sisters been taken from me permanently, I don't know how I'd react, but it wouldn't be good.

"The Grunch killed them?" he echoed.

"They were outnumbered by my count. My guess is they ambushed your friends the way they did my sisters and me. Clay came in and spoiled the fun for us, though. Although it was entertaining to watch him explode a tree with one of them."

"It was a fair fight when I—I had to get Theia to safety, my instincts kicked in and I had no control—" Jackson's voice was hollow as he just sat there.

"When we get back to the swamp, we can hunt down every last Grunch in the area. I get it." Ella looked directly at him, her impassive face showing more understanding than I'd seen in centuries. "Thank you for getting my sister out of harm's way."

The ping of Fin's cell phone broke the silence. He pulled it out and frowned at the screen. "It's from Nia." He looked up at Jackson. "She says to tell you not to do anything stupid before she gets here tomorrow, and she's bringing your phone."

"Tell the Priestess I don't need her spell," Jackson said with a glance at me.

"Wait, you know that pain in the ass?" Ella asked.

"Yes."

"Is this the same Priestess who gave you the ingredients for the severing spell?" I asked Jackson. He'd never told me her name, but I was even more confused by the fact that Ella seemed to know her.

271

"Yes." He sat back and looked at my sister and Fin. "How do you know her?"

"She's been helping us track you," Fin said, glancing suspiciously between Ella and Jackson. "You said she gave you a list of ingredients; that wouldn't happen to be the one with Gorgone scales and other odd things, now would it?"

"How do you know about that?" Jackson bristled.

"Why was my sister's blood all over that safehouse of yours?" Ella cut in, rage flickering over her features.

My brows knotted together, and I tried to remember why my blood would be in a safehouse. "Shit. You found the safehouse where I ripped my vocal cords out."

All eyes were on me now, except Jackson, who was watching the rest of the table like he was about to fight with them any moment.

"Don't look at me like that. You cut your own throat every night to deal with the itch." I jabbed a finger in Ella's direction.

"Fair. I don't do that anymore. Fin has solved the issue."

"Wait, Nia has been helping you track me since the beginning?" Jackson demanded.

"Pretty close to the beginning. We found her shop after we found that list," Fin explained.

272

"And the bitch sent us on a wild goose chase," Ella seethed.

"What kind of game is she playing?" Jackson growled.

—**Ping**—

All eyes fell on Fin as he opened the text. "It says: Congratulations on the pregnancy, and thank you for getting the ingredients. Sit tight and don't do anything stupid, any of you. I'll be there tomorrow evening with answers. I still think a ball gag would have been entertaining." Fin looked up at Jackson, who had the decency to look embarrassed. "I don't think I even want to know about that last one."

"No, I think I wanna know about this ball gag." I crossed my arms and pinned Jackson with a stern look. Had he and the Priestess been intimate?

Jackson cleared his throat and glanced around the table before answering. "She said it would work just as well as the collar."

"The shock collar you put on my sister?" Ella cut in.

"For fuck's sake, what is wrong with all of you?" Kassie demanded, looking around the table.

"If I had to guess, I'd say our 'not a masochist' sister is indeed a masochist." Ella calmly took a bite of her spaghetti as she held my gaze.

273

"Fuck you." I could feel my face heating at her accusation, the memory of Jackson spanking me just before dinner still fresh in my mind.

"She's a brat, not a masochist," Jackson interjected without looking at me.

"Not helping," I muttered.

"Anyway, what do you think Nia is planning?" Kassie asked, redirecting the conversation.

"Let's see, she sent us across the country to get ingredients for what she claims is a severing spell and claimed to help you track us. Now she's telling us to sit tight and congratulating us on my pregnancy." I thought for a moment, running it all through my head. "Wait, were you the ones tracking the Jeep?"

"Yes, all the way to Illinois. It looked like you were in the passenger seat on several of the camera feeds we found," Fin said as he shifted uncomfortably and glanced at Ella.

I rolled my eyes. "Marcus replaced me with a blow-up doll and some sort of spell. He's Nia's brother, apparently. Gods, this is so fucked up."

"So we have a brother and sister team who can cast spells and they have the ability to see the future. I should probably

274

contact the agency on this one," Fin said as he pulled out his phone.

"Nia was listed with mine," Jackson interjected.

"Are you insisting she's safe then?" Fin asked, his phone still in hand.

"No. I'm saying we can't trust anyone."

—Ping—

Everyone looked at Fin. His jaw twitched before he opened the message and read it aloud. "Severing spells won't work on mate bonds, but they work on powers—even those of a God. A father-daughter reunion is in order. See you tomorrow."

Chapter 25

Theia...

Morning had crept in slowly and softly, the silence hanging heavy in the safehouse. None of us had slept well, I was sure of it. Jackson had been awake every time I'd rolled over. Now we all sat on the porch as a light mist came down, casting the evening in shades of grey that allowed Fin out even though it wasn't yet dark.

Jackson was sitting on the steps with his back to the post, and I was sitting between his legs with my back against his chest. He'd hardly stopped touching me all day, like he was afraid to let me out of his reach. His fingers brushed over my neck, tickling the bite mark he'd left on me two days ago. I'd since learned that it would scar and never fade that he'd marked me as his mate for all to see.

Sitting there, listening to the distant crash of the waves, felt odd. This little moment of peace was charged with tension.

We'd all made our speculations on what the Priestess had meant by a father-daughter reunion, and nothing we came up with was good. The fact that I was now pregnant only added more frustration, as it was five against one that I should sit this out.

"What are you thinking about, brat?"

"Murder," I muttered.

"Funny, me too," Ella echoed from the left. I glanced over to see her methodically moving a blade over a sharpening stone.

"When are you not thinking about murder, Ella?" Kassie asked.

"When I'm fucking Fin."

"That's a relief," Fin muttered, shifting uncomfortably.

I tilted my head and just looked at her. "Who are you and what have you done with my sister?"

"We have company," Jackson growled behind me.

We stood, and all of us slowly walked off the porch to the figure standing halfway between the house and the ocean. As we neared, I could clearly make out his rugged features, dark brown beard, and the sunbaked tone of his skin. The scent of tobacco and driftwood wafted in the breeze.

"Hello, daughters," Ares said as he stood on the beach. "I think it's about time we have a little chat about how you've been handling things."

277

"How have we been handling things? What the fuck is that supposed to mean?" I snapped, staring at the male who'd spent the last 12,000 years tormenting us, the male who'd whispered in Hitler's ear, who'd pushed and manipulated us like his own little personal playthings into bloody battle after bloody battle.

"Theia, my mouthy little scrapper, I am very disappointed in you." He shook his finger at me like a parent scolding a small child. "I hadn't expected it after the way you handled the Grunch I sent to you, but when the Lycans showed up, you left yourself wide open and went down without even killing one of them. I even sent extra Grunch to make it more entertaining, a little horde of bloodthirsty creatures that attack without allegiance."

"You what?" Kassie demanded, stepping forward, Clay grabbing her arm to keep her by his side.

"I should have known. All the years we lived there, it makes sense that you were the one to send those fuckers after us," Ella said, her voice dripping with more disdain than I'd heard in thousands of years.

"And you, Lycan, I thought I'd convinced your kind to wage war on them, and yet here you are, drooling over the daughter of Ares like a strip of bacon," Ares went on, beginning to pace the beach, his hands clasped behind his back.

I turned to look at Jackson, only to see his eyes had turned golden, his Wolf lingering just beneath the surface. I turned back to Ares. "What do you mean, you convinced them to wage war on us?" I demanded as a strange static seemed to fill the air.

"Not him—them," Ares said as he waved a dismissive hand. "Human wars are so boring. All the weapons and gadgets they have, where is the real fight, you know?" He shrugged.

"Then I had the idea of an immortal war, one that the three of you would head with a bloodthirsty savagery to make your old man proud." He shook his fist in front of him, a serious look on his face.

His tone turned passive. "It wasn't too hard. Most immortals are too stupid to realize that Sirens don't use their gifts unless they have to, not since getting off that island Poseidon had them stranded on. A few well-placed rumors, and the Lycan pack was ready to end the 'threat' to their precious mating bond. As though such a thing were more entertaining than the delightful carnage of battle." The way he'd said mating bond in a mocking tone made my anger flare even more.

"If carnage is what you want, why have you been hiding from us all these millennia?" Ella played with her switchblade, a darkness in her eyes I hadn't seen since Troy, her stance predatory.

"Easy, Songbird, you're getting worked up," Fin said as he put his hands in his pockets, a seemingly relaxed stance, but we all knew he'd put daggers in each one earlier.

I could hear the low rumble of growls coming from Jackson and Clay, the anger and tension emanating from all of us charging the air.

"Theia, why don't you go inside while I speak with your father?" Jackson's voice was distorted, his Wolf struggling to surface, his fingertips already forming claws.

"Not until I remove his head from his body," I said coldly.

"He is not your father, but mine. Hermes, messenger of the Gods and trickster," Nia said, startling us as she came out of a portal with two Lycan males behind her who looked suspiciously like Jackson. "And the Pack Leaders just heard every word you said." She set down a basket in front of her and calmly began pulling items out. "Are you going to drop the glamour, or will I have to force you to drop it?"

Pack Leaders? Shit, was one of them Jackson's father? I spared them one last glance before turning back to the male who I'd thought was my father.

Ares changed from the well-built, gruff-looking male into a smallish, yet athletically built one.

280

"I really have been improving them all these years. Ares, however, has been an absent father since before they left the island." He adjusted his stance and as a breeze carried the new scent of driftwood and coffee; his true scent.

"Theia, I'll keep his head for you to play with later. Listen to your male," Kassie said as she edged forward, Clay staying right with her.

"See, that fire, right there! Where was that when I sent you those Lycans? My beautiful little killers. None of you truly want me dead. I've made you what you are. Don't you see? I've kept you from getting weak, like your mother and her wretched sisters."

Kassie and I glanced at each other, but not Ella. Her eyes never left him.

"You've kept us from becoming weak?" I asked in an incredulous tone, ignoring the near-constant growling from Jackson, whose hand was placed protectively on my abdomen.

"You destroyed every corner of peace we've ever found," Kassie raged. "And what do you know about our mother and aunts?"

A strange shadow crossed his face.

"She was the most beautiful of them all, you know. I'd been thinking of how to get her off that island without Poseidon

281

knowing. Then she went and got herself pregnant by Ares. Mortals I could forgive—we outlive them, after all—but Ares? I've always *hated* him."

"You visited Ella in the gladiator pits before she was ever even immortal, and you left her there!" The rage filling my body was more than I could take. He'd said our father was absent before we even left the island? How long had he been watching us?

"And look how strong she's become." He gestured to her. "You—I thought after your child was killed, you'd wage a war that lasted decades! Instead, you just cried and begged Poseidon to bring him back. *Pathetic*," he spat, hatred lacing his voice. "Your vengeance was so weak, just like *Ares*. If you were truly my daughters, you'd have figured it out, how to escape, how to save that child before it died. Look at Nia; she's done wonders."

"Do not ever compare me to you," Nia said with venom. She snapped her fingers, and a candle lit at her feet. She picked up a large jar and swirled it around. "I'm more like my mother than I am you. I don't disguise myself and pretend to be another God to gain power or vengeance." She dipped a string into the jar. If I had to guess, the jar was full of the ingredients Jackson and I had gathered.

282

She smiled then and looked at him. "There is one thing we share, *Father*. DNA." She spit on the candle, then dropped the string into the flame and began to chant words that made no sense to me.

"What are you doing?" Hermes demanded as he fell back a step.

She let out a hiss and made a jerky wave of her hand over the candle, and the flame stopped flickering despite the breeze and mist on the Washington shoreline. "Severing you from your power to travel. Shame, too, because it means I can't travel either until the candle burns out." She turned and looked at the Lycan to her left. "He would see your grandchildren dead, the two inside her belly right now." Nia pointed at me, her black polish glinting in the dimming light.

"What are you going to do about it?"

One heartbeat, then two, and all hell broke loose. A low snarl ripped from Jackson's throat. His wolf-human hybrid form tore out of him, the primal part clawing its way up from his very bones.

His clothing tore, and bones cracked audibly next to me. He launched himself forward, and not far behind him, two more Lycans charged at Hermes.

Hermes roared as his form flickered, but didn't leave. He was severed from his ability, but not his strength.

As one Lycan latched onto his arm, Hermes flung him off, sending him skidding across the wet sand. I went to move forward and join, only to have Clay lift me into his arms without warning. He spun around and rushed me back toward the Priestess, even as I felt him shifting into his Sasquatch form, his clothing shredding around us.

"Damn it! I can fight!"

"Stay with me, I need your strength to hold the flame," Nia said as she held out a hand to me.

I hesitated only a moment before taking her hand. I could feel the immediate pull on my aura, my strength shifting and twisting around us to create an invisible barrier. My knees buckled, and I hit the sand next to Nia before I felt a wave of warmth spread through me, and some of my energy returned. I could feel it, pushing and pulling like the tide.

My gaze fell back on the battle. Blood colored the shore as Hermes flung off his opponents. I watched with my heart in my throat as Ella stabbed her switchblade into the side of his neck before being knocked backward. Golden blood spurted from his wound.

Kassie executed a spin-kick that nearly hit him in the face before his hand caught her ankle, yanking her off the ground. He flung her like a ragdoll, but before she could hit the ground, Fin caught her, staggering under the force but keeping them both upright. He set her down and, in a flash, was slicing the back of Hermes' right knee.

"You think you're warriors," Hermes spat, twisting away from him, "but you're tools. All of you. Broken toys sharpened by rage. I shaped you."

"You shaped *nothing*," Kassie snapped, launching forward with the blades she'd had stored in her boots. She stabbed downward, not to kill, but to wound. To make him bleed. To humiliate him. "We shaped ourselves surviving you."

Hermes caught her wrist and flung her backward, but Clay was already dragging him down again, driving his forearm into Hermes' throat.

Clay charged forward with a roar of rage in his Sasquatch form.

The ground trembled beneath his feet as he slammed into Hermes, knocking the God off balance with sheer weight and fury. It was like watching a tree uproot itself and decide to go on a hunt. Hermes crashed onto the sand, snarling, but not in pain. In disbelief.

285

Clay launched a fist into the side of Hermes' chest. The messenger God buckled on one side before he righted himself, dodged a blow from Clay, and swerved out of the way of Jackson. The other two Lycans lunged at him, and he launched a blow into the chest of one but was unable to block the other. Another roar of pain erupted from him and mingled with the yelp of the Lycan he'd struck.

Next to me, Nia continued to chant. As I glanced at the candle, I saw that it was burning faster than a normal candle. If I had to guess, I would say that the candle would be completely burned out in less than thirty minutes. Looking back at the fight, I had to wonder—would that be long enough? Even with the odds stacked seven to one, Hermes was holding his own, moving with surprising agility even with the wounds he'd sustained.

Behind them, the candle flared blue. Nia's voice rose with it, the spell reaching some kind of climax. Each word she chanted felt as if it were etched directly into my bones.

Hermes screamed. His face twisted. Not in fear but in fury.

And then he moved.

He was fast, so fast I didn't even see the shift in weight before he was in motion. One second he was on the sand, and the next he was a blur of divine rage, slamming into Clay, sending the Bigfoot shifter sprawling into the surf with a sickening thud.

Jackson roared, lunging, but Hermes was already gone, dodging, weaving, his movements impossibly precise. He struck Fin next, elbowing him in the throat hard enough to drop him to one knee. Kassie slashed at him with her blade, but he caught her wrist mid-swing, twisted it until she cried out, and threw her bodily into Clay's still-recovering form.

"You think you've won?!" he screamed, his voice ragged. "You think removing one piece of my power makes you safe? You've only cornered the serpent!"

He appeared in front of me—too fast. I didn't even have time to blink before Jackson collided with him mid-lunge, snarling, claws catching Hermes across the chest.

Hermes rolled with the impact, blood spraying in arcs of gold, and slammed his foot into Jackson's ribs, knocking him sideways.

But that small moment—that flash of distraction—was all Ella needed.

She walked toward him calmly. No rage on her face. No joy.

Just certainty.

287

"You know what the pits taught me?" she said, voice cold and quiet. "I enjoy spilling the blood of males."

Hermes turned fast, but not fast enough.

She was already on him.

One blade to the thigh, severing his balance.

Another to his side, just under the ribs. She left it there.

And then, with a smooth, almost loving motion, she slid a third blade straight into his throat.

He gurgled—eyes wide, mouth working, fingers clawing at the wound like he could undo it.

"You didn't make me," she whispered, pressing in close. "But you sure as hell made me hate you."

She twisted the blade.

Hermes dropped to his knees.

Kassie came up behind him, the machete she'd had strapped to her back in hand. With one lethal swing, Hermes' head toppled and his body fell to the sand.

And he didn't rise again.

For a long moment, no one spoke. The wind picked up again, the mist thickening, the candle's white flame guttering down into nothing.

288

I looked down at the blood on the sand—golden, divine, and ugly. Then up at my sisters. At the males who'd stood with us.

Nia let go of my hand and reached into her basket again, pulling out the feathers Jackson and I had gathered. "It's time to finish this."

I followed her to the fallen God who'd tormented us for so long. The male who'd paraded himself as our father and shattered every delicate moment we'd forged for ourselves. She handed a feather to each of us. "Together, we burn him," she said calmly.

"I don't know if you realize this or not, but these are feathers," Ella said in a bland tone.

"Phoenix feathers," I clarified.

Nia smiled. "And one little word will ignite them, and their magical fire will incinerate even a God. Each of us will touch one feather to him, wherever you like. Then we add the head."

We moved as one.

Ella pressed her feather to his shoulder. Kassie to the open gash on his side. I stepped in and touched mine to his wrist, the veins there still pulsing faintly like he couldn't accept he'd already died.

289

Nia leaned down last, placing hers to the center of his chest.

"Ignite." Nia's voice held a power that ripped through the mist and sent a shiver up my spine.

The feathers shimmered, then flared—bright white, red, and violet flames curling outward like wings unfurling. For a second, nothing happened. Then Hermes's body spasmed once—twice—before the fire caught and swallowed him whole.

Jackson handed me the head as the blaze continued.

"Asshole," I muttered as I glared at the dead, unseeing eyes before dropping it into the flames.

The God who had caused so much pain, so many scars, vanished without a sound as the fire consumed faster and faster until there was nothing left.

Ash drifted into the wind, gold and gray.

And it was done.

Chapter 26

Theia...

What now?

The question hung between us as we all sat inside the safehouse in the numb aftermath of the battle.

Who would have thought that twelve thousand years of hunting Ares—blaming him for every torment, every lost chance at happiness, every shattered moment of peace—would end on a rain-soaked beach in Washington on December 14th, only to discover it had been Hermes all along? He had worn Ares' face like a mask and manipulated the truth until no one could decipher it.

Jackson held me in his arms and stared at the two Lycans having a silent conversation in the kitchen as we sat on the couch. They'd been using sign language and quickly moved to another room where we couldn't watch their discussion.

Clay and Kassie sat on the other end of the couch from Jackson and me, while Ella and Fin sat in the recliner. Seeing Ella cuddled up with a male was still unsettling for me. Even with Helen, she hadn't cuddled that much, at least not in front of others, due to Helen's need to appear as a loving wife to her husband.

"What do you think they are talking about?" I asked Jackson, my attention falling to the Lycans.

"You and your sisters. We've been hunting Sirens for over a century because of Hermes' manipulation. Our packs have killed your kind without just cause. There is a lot to discuss, and a lot to atone for." Jackson's tone was low and heavy. He slipped his hand onto my stomach. "The future is here, though. You are my mate, and our children will help the others see the truth."

"How will our children do that? Will they be in danger?" The thought of losing my children sent me into an immediate panic. My heart was pounding painfully, and I was struggling to breathe as I clutched my stomach.

"No one will harm our children—or you. I swear it." His arms tightened protectively around me.

"They will have to go through all of us to get to you," Clay added.

"Indeed. And considering we just took down a God, I'd say we are more than capable of protecting you should the need arise," Fin said calmly.

"That won't be necessary," one of the males from the kitchen stated. Maybe his name was Mika? Or was it Waya?

"Per our traditions, once you've found your mate, you may assume leadership of the pack. Your mother will need to educate and help guide your mate," the other one said as he leaned against the doorframe. He tilted his head and looked at me. "Our packs have a lot to learn about your kind. I hope that you will not hold our shortcomings against us."

I glanced at Jackson before looking back at the male. "We were all manipulated. The things Hermes did are going to make it hard for everyone, but trust is earned."

"Mika, it looks like you have a very wise daughter-in-law," Waya said with a smile as he clapped his brother on the back.

"Are you saying my sister is going to be the wife of the Alpha?" Kassie asked.

"Yes. She will have an equal position at the head of the pack. I'd like to invite all of you to assist in the transition away from the path we've been on." Mika moved into the living room and took a seat in the empty chair that remained. He looked at everyone in the room. "There is a lot of trust that needs to be built, but based on what we've seen, and what we recorded thanks to Nia's instruction, I think we can get things moving."

Nia, the Priestess, who had actively guided us to the annihilation of her own father. She'd guided Jackson and me to collect the items for the spell that would keep him from traveling away via portal, and the feathers that held the power to incinerate a God. When Kassie had asked her why she'd helped us, she'd said her fate was intertwined with ours since the day she was born and that she had more answers to find. After that, she'd stepped through a portal and disappeared, the candle flame gone and her abilities returned.

Jackson's hand was still on my stomach, warm and steady. For once, the silence wasn't suffocating. It was full of grief, hope, of things reborn, and things lost.

In the flickering shadows of the safehouse, with the rain still falling outside in the black of night, I realized something I hadn't dared to believe in for a long time:

We were *safe*.

For now, we could breathe.

For the first time in twelve thousand years, we had a chance to be *happy*.

Epilogue

Nia knew her spell would have a cost, but not what that cost would be...

As Marcus stepped into his hotel room in Illinois, the scent of smoke hit him first—sharp, clean, and rising from the calm form of Amani. Wisps curled upward from her plumage, blue, red, and gold feathers catching fire in slow, mesmerizing waves. She didn't scream. She didn't flinch. Instead, the Phoenix gazed at her igniting form with wide-eyed awe, then tilted her head back and stretched her wings to their full span, welcoming the blaze. Flames surged across her body... then flickered and died. The fire sputtered out with a reluctant hiss, her feathers untouched. Amani blinked and looked at herself, waiting for that moment of rebirth that never came. Her eyes met Marcus's across the room, confusion swirling in their depths as he breathed one word:

295

"Curious."

***

At 4:32 p.m. PST on the shore in Washington State, the candle flickered to life, a charge going through the air as magic rippled out—everything came with a price.

At 5:31 p.m. MST, somewhere in Colorado, hooves thrummed against the earth as the mighty Centaur ran across the open land, wind tugging at his human hair. His breath frosted before him as his lungs filled with the December evening air. At 5:32 p.m., his hooves struck the earth once more in Colorado, and then the expanse of Greece was before him—his sudden change in location unexpected, leaving his head spinning.

***

Washington was a nice, quiet place for the Ogre family. They made their living mostly from the potato farm they owned, but this time of year, they harvested their earwax and formed magical candles for the Immortal community. The family was just heating some of the wax they had collected when a wave of energy washed over them—it felt like a rollercoaster for a moment—and then wax began leaking from all their ears as the grandfather clock chimed 4:32 p.m.

***

Kansas wasn't the best place to live, but Deedra had found her own purpose here, hiding her appearance from Mortals and shielding males from her gaze. At 6:31 p.m. CST, she walked into her home after a long day. At 6:32 p.m., her snakes hissed, suddenly shedding all at once. The sting of the spell to conceal them was intense on their fresh and sensitive scales. She gasped at the sudden sensation, not sure what had just happened.

***

At 6:31 p.m. CST, Lola was just pulling on her boots to head out. She was taking the night off work. All the shit last month with the Priestess and other Immortals had left her drained and irritated. At 6:32 p.m., she opened her front door, and as she stepped out into the Texas heat, she was suddenly thrust into a chilled city with cobbled streets and imposing buildings of immaculate stone.

***

All was quiet and cold in the weeping waters. The creature lurked, waiting for someone to join in the sweet sorrow of its depths. Then, something unexpected happened. At 6:32 p.m. CST, a ripple of energy—a severing of something powerful—flowed through the waters and caused the creature to open its eyes and looked about. Where had that come from? Had someone used its power? Clever someone. Would they feed its

297

never-ending thirst for sorrow? The desire sent shivers of anticipation through the creature that ebbed out in a great wave through the waterways, stretching to the oceans beyond.

Thank you for reading! For more updates and books by Ruth Nalio or signed copies go to www.authorruthnalio.com and for a collection of indie authors and their works across multiple genres visit www.indiebackbooks.com and happy reading!